A Collection of
Whimsical
Fables

A Nymph's Tale

A Zimbell House Anthology

A Nymph's Tale

A Collection
of
Whimsical Fables

A Zimbell House Anthology

ZIMBELL HOUSE
PUBLISHING
UNION LAKE, MICHIGAN

"Attention: Permissions Coordinator"
Zimbell House Publishing, LLC
PO Box 1172
Union Lake, Michigan 48387
mail to: info@zimbellhousepublishing.com

© 2018 Zimbell House Publishing, LLC

Published in the United States by Zimbell House Publishing
http://www.ZimbellHousePublishing.com

All Rights Reserved

Trade Paper ISBN: 978-1-947210-19-6
Kindle ISBN: 978-1-947210-20-2
Digital ISBN: 978-1-947210-21-9
Library of Congress Control Number: 2018900697

First Edition: February 2018
10 9 8 7 6 5 4 3 2 1

ZIMBELL HOUSE PUBLISHING
UNION LAKE

Acknowledgements

Zimbell House Publishing would like to thank all those that contributed to this anthology. We chose to showcase nine new voices that best represented our vision for this work.

We would also like to thank our Zimbell House team for all their hard work and dedication to these projects.

Table of Contents

The Wingless Faerie

EZEKIEL O. TRACY

The morning sun rose over the horizon bringing with it a fresh breath of wind and light that shone on every part of the meadow. Dew drops found their place on the blades of grass and on the edge of leaves as the day began anew. Bumblebees woke from their slumber and rose steadily into the air from their hives, setting out to find the best pollen of the day.

Flowers opened across the meadow as if on cue when graced by beams of light. Slowly each petal unfolded, presenting itself to the world and waking the occupants nestled comfortably within. The faeries of the field unfurled themselves from their sleeping positions, stretching their arms and giving hearty yawns as the day began around them. Birds took flight, finding food for their chicks, butterflies flapped lazily from one morning glory to the next, eating their fill of breakfast, and chipmunks darted to and fro, collecting and storing the nuts that had fallen from trees during the night.

The faeries let their wings wake up, giving slow, deliberate movements to their paper-thin appendages. Each faerie took great pride in their wings. One could have wings of a dragonfly, while another faerie could look to have wings of a hummingbird. They were all unique and precious. A faerie that didn't take care of their wings was frowned upon, for their wings made them who they were.

As they woke, a faerie with wings of pure white with black dots jumped from her flower and arched her back.

With her wings on full display, the faerie soared to the ground and began the day's work. All around the meadow faeries followed suit. They began helping animals around the glen, repairing leaves that were torn, picking up twigs and animal fur to give to the birds for their nests. The sun shone down on the clearing in the forest as the creatures basked in its glory and did good work.

The white-winged faerie walked on the ground, picking up twigs and building small piles of dead leaves for the animals to rummage through when she spotted something peculiar. There, at the base of a vivid red Zinnia, sat a basket. Finding a basket was not a foreign surprise in the meadow. The faeries wove them and used them for carrying things, but this basket, in particular, had a hood that covered the top. She walked to the base of the flower and looked into the tan, woven container. Inside, swaddled in a soft leaf, a small baby moved. The faerie took one look at the babe and gathered the basket in her arms. Faerie children were meant for the nursery where it was warm until their wings grew in. She swiftly and frantically flew the basket to the willow tree on the edge of the meadow, drawing the gaze of everyone she passed.

Fluttering to a halt inside the tree, the faerie found her way to the center, where other faerie children lay in their baskets sleeping, or cooing about. She found an open spot in the nursery and set the basket down, hoping that the babe hadn't been outside for too long. The baby faeries were taken outside once a day at the hottest point so that they could experience what the world looked and felt like. It occurred to the white-winged faerie that this youngling could have been outside all night, by itself, having been forgotten when the rest were brought in.

She watched as the baby faerie slept, worry creeping into her mind and settling on her soul.

※ ※

Ryker woke up with the sun and waited for her flower to open. She sat patiently at first but soon was overcome by the need to move. At the first twitch of the petals, the faerie girl pushed through and slid down the stalk. She didn't have time to watch as everyone else woke up and fluttered to the ground, today was the day she would fly.

The young faerie ran to the base of an oak tree, pushing open the door and hurried in. A small table had been set up, and on it, a variety of bits and pieces made themselves at home. She quickly gathered the supplies she needed and rushed onward, back outside and towards the boulder.

The boulder was near the center of the meadow. It gave shade when shade was needed, and was a place of gathering when the faeries wanted to enjoy each other's company. Today it would be the place that Ryker flew.

She raced across the ground, paying no attention to the faeries that fluttered around her, pushing through patches of grass until she found herself face to face with the boulder. Climbing swiftly, yet carefully, the faerie made her way to the top where she marveled at the expanse of the meadow. This sight took her breath away nearly every time. She stood for only a second before she strapped the twigs and leaves to her back and slid her arms into their spots. The wingless faerie now had wings and was determined to be like her brothers and sisters. Ryker took a few steps back and raced forward. She felt the breeze in her makeshift wings, and her heart beat quickly as her feet began to lift off the rock. Space opened beneath her as she took flight, soaring above the flowers of the meadow.

The white-winged faerie found her place beside Ryker, with a small grin. The two faeries sailed for a short distance until Ryker had to flap the wings she had made for herself. The force of pushing down and pulling up was nearly too much for her arms and the twigs that framed her leaf-wings. A small cracking noise came from her left and she watched as one of the twigs snapped in half, leaving her with only one workable wing.

The white-winged faerie fluttered above Ryker and grabbed her by the waist, helping the youngling to float down to the ground.

Ryker tore the contraption off of her back and felt tears welling in her eyes. She only wanted to be like the others. The stumps on her back, where no wings had grown, reminded her of her difference, and it ached her to the core.

Soma, the white-winged faerie, sat with Ryker as she cried. Ryker turned her face toward the sun and looked at the broken pieces of the wings she wanted desperately to have. The day was fresh and new, and she would try again.

Before she could stand, Soma grabbed Ryker's hand and pulled her up. They had work to do first. The meadow depended on the faeries to keep it healthy and clean. Soma lifted off into the air, with Ryker running beneath her. The wingless faerie raced through the undergrowth faster than any faerie could fly, and she was standing before the nettle bush before Soma landed. The two worked together to guide the nettles around the glen. They acted as a protective barrier from any foul predators or humans who might seek to disrupt the peaceful patch in the woods.

As they worked, Soma carefully moved one branch at a time, conscious of her wings and the damage the thin needles of the plant could do to them.

Ryker, on the other hand, grabbed armfuls at a time, maneuvering as much of the plant as she could, with the only worry being her arms getting pricked or her hair becoming entangled. The two worked together, swiftly completing the task at hand. As it came to an end, a group of faeries Ryker's age appeared and threw her makeshift wings in front of her. They pointed at the faerie and laughed, the sound of chimes echoing from their mouths as she stood with her brow furrowed.

Soma shooed the faerie bullies away and went to counsel Ryker, who pushed past the white-winged faerie, stomping back to the oak tree. The girl would fly. She would show them that she was like them. Soma watched as Ryker walked away, sadness burrowing into her soul. She remembered the day she had found Ryker outside under that Zinnia flower. Soma had sat with the baby Ryker for days as her brothers and sisters in the nursery had grown wings. The faerie who had been forgotten outside had begun to show growth, but nothing came of it, save the stumps on her back.

Together they had watched the other faeries take flight. Learning how to maneuver on the breeze, while Ryker ran underneath them, wishing and dreaming of being in the air. The young faerie would jump from stones, urging the stumps on her back to beat but they were still. Time and time again Ryker had tried to fly, but the outcome was always the same. Her brothers and sisters soon saw the difference between themselves and their wingless sister. Their wings gave them pride and a faerie with no wings must certainly be beneath them. The taunts had erupted from the group, causing the young Ryker to run and hide. A swift anger had filled Soma, and she quickly dispelled the jeering crowd.

From that moment on, Ryker had been determined to have wings and to show them she was just as much a faerie as they. If Soma had counted correctly, this had been the twenty-first attempt at flying. Each time the young faerie got closer and closer to achieving her goal but never was satisfied. The white-winged faerie watched Ryker enter the oak tree and then took flight herself, there was work to be done, and she could smell rain coming.

The wingless faerie shut the oak tree door behind her and went to work. She had drawn up each pair of wings and now looked over her sketches, trying to determine where she had gone wrong. Adding a fix here and there, the young faerie began to work again. In the little room, she had collected twigs, blades of grass, leaves, and many other items to help her build her wings. As she went to work, she grabbed various things. She used to twigs to build a frame, then tied them together with the blades of grass. When the frame was fastened together, the girl brought thin but sturdy leaves to the table and placed them on the frame. Carefully, she used sap to glue the leaves into place. By the time her project was complete, the sun was setting, and Ryker had to hurry to make it to her flower before it closed for the night.

She raced to the base of her plant and swiftly climbed to the petals as they began to close. She nestled inside, comfortably curling into a ball and watched as the flower closed around her. Looking into the sky, she saw the first stars begin to pepper the night. The faerie fell asleep but was awoken by the wind. A powerful breeze had picked up, blowing her flower to and fro. The soft thumping of raindrops filled the meadow, which quickly grew to steady drumming as the storm increased. With little warning, the petals to her home were ripped off, sending the faerie tumbling to the hard ground.

Rivers of water flowed around her as she tried to stand. The drops of water were hard and fast, pounding the small faerie into the ground. She looked around her and saw many of her brothers and sisters in the same situation. Forcing herself up, Ryker ran in between the raindrops to the cover of a bush. She stood catching her breath when she saw a flash of white.

Holding onto her flower, Soma dangled in the air as the wind blew fiercely and the rain pelted her. Her wings hung limply on her back, and the older faerie was seconds from losing her grip. Ryker took action. She raced through the rain, trying her best to ignore the pounding of the rain as it found its way onto her back. When she got to Soma's flower, she clawed her way up its slick surface. As she held onto the stem, Soma's grip failed her, and the white-winged faerie fell through the open space. Ryker wrapped her legs tightly around the flower and let go with her hands, reaching as far as she could, grabbing for Soma's hands.

The faerie made contact and held onto the older faerie as the force of her fall slid Ryker down the stalk. They landed on the wet earth, wind disappearing from their lungs, and lay there as the rain continued to pour. Throughout the meadow, other faeries raced to find cover as their wings dangled from their backs, useless.

Soma and Ryker stood. One with wings crumpled and soaked, and the other with legs tired and sore. They helped each other to the bush and sat, soon falling asleep as the torrent of water continued to fall from the sky.

When they awoke, the glen that they so lovingly protected and nurtured was in disrepair. Very few flowers had survived the night, while branches from the trees that surrounded their home had snapped and fallen. Great streams and ponds of water now made their way into the meadow. The earth was rough and small valleys peppered the once smooth dirt.

The faeries walked from under their protective coverings, looking around themselves and feeling a sense of dread. All of their hard work had disappeared in a night. The guards they had put in place to protect the meadow were beaten down and broken. The homes of so many of their animal friends were thrown from the trees and bushes they had chosen carefully. The sun was rising on the meadow, and with it, a new sorrow that seemed to flow as freely as the streams of water that cut through the ground.

Having nowhere else to go, Ryker and Soma made their way to the boulder. It sat solid and steady, having been undamaged by the wind and the rain. Branches and twigs had been blown against the great rock, and they now sat at its feet, broken and twisted. A small pond of water rested nearby with leaves floated on its surface. Ryker touched the surface of the boulder and felt a sense of calmness enter her body.

They could rebuild. They could start from the beginning. Soma stood beside the wingless faerie as their brothers and sisters found their way to the boulder. They stood around lost and hopeless, wings wet, drooping off their backs. With determination, Ryker turned from the crowd that quickly gathered and grabbed a twig that rested against the giant stone. She pulled it from its place and started to walk to the edge of the meadow, where she dropped it and went back for another.

Thrice she went to and from the monolith, until Soma joined her, grabbing a bigger stick that required them both to carry. The crowd of faeries, whose sadness and doubt had filled the space before, soon began to see the work being done to clear their meadow. Slowly at first, faeries here and there began to pick up sticks, or smooth over the ground. Starting where they stood and expanding their reach, this small section of the meadow was soon transformed into its old self. The ground was pushed back into place, twigs and branches were used to build new walls along the edges, new flowers were planted and old ones repaired as best as they could be, with Ryker leading the way.

When the patch was to their liking, the faeries ran off to different sections of the meadow. Many of their wings were still drying, but a few faeries were able to take flight. Those faeries in the sky served as scouts, flying high to see where the most damage had taken place. A couple of faeries ran to check on the nursery, while others searched out their friends, the woodland creatures. The meadow was soon thrumming with activity as animals joined the fray, moving what they could and rebuilding their nests to the best of their ability.

Soma was stretching her wings, testing them for stability and dryness when she saw on the edge of the meadow, a face peering out from behind the leaf of a bush. The face quickly hid from the older faerie, but curiosity got the best of her. The white-winged faerie cautiously walked towards the bush. She could hear nothing to give her a clue that someone was hiding there, but she carefully pushed aside a leaf and looked in. There sitting clustered together under the branches and leaves of the bush, was the group of Ryker's siblings. They huddled together and seemed to be shivering. That's when she saw the most terrible sight. Dangling lifeless off their backs, were their wings.

Looking shredded and torn, the once beautiful wings of the younger faeries hung useless. They cowered together, obviously wishing to remain hidden from the world. Their pride wounded and their lives forever altered, these faeries were living in shame. Soma stepped back and away from the bush. By this time, her own wings were good as new, and she took flight. Soaring above the meadow, she quickly found Ryker helping a squirrel collect acorns that had fallen from their place in the trees. Soma landed nearby and lent a hand until the acorns were picked up and on their way to the squirrels hiding place. Ryker stood smiling as the squirrel left.

The older faerie grabbed the girl's hand and began to guide her to the bush. Feeling that something was wrong or out of place, Ryker picked up her speed and was soon dragging Soma along behind her. Letting her strong legs carry her, the wingless faerie came to a halt when Soma tapped her hand. Walking gingerly, the white-winged faerie made her way to the bush, motioning Ryker to her side. Together they pulled back a leaf and saw the display before them. Ryker wheeled backward, with her hand covering her mouth. At first, Soma believed the other faerie to be gasping in surprise, but the sound of chimes came from behind the hand.

Ryker laughed at the other faeries. She laughed because now they were the same. They would know her struggle and feel a pain deeper than they had ever known with their wings in shreds. The first wingless faerie ran from that spot, laughter falling behind her, desperate to show off her siblings who were no longer as beautiful as they once were. Soma followed close behind in the air. She soared quickly diving at the girl and pinning her to the ground.

The meadow was in repair and joy was filling the air, but the space between Soma and Ryker filled with sadness and regret. There had been a thought in Soma's mind that Ryker would have wanted to help her brothers and sisters, but now the young faerie reveled in their despair. She relished the fact that they were even now. It frightened Soma. This girl whom she had walked beside was a creature she barely recognized.

Ryker pushed and struggled to stand; wanting to spread the news that she was no longer the only wingless faerie. She wanted the pain of her siblings to be in the open so that they might be as ridiculed as she was. Using her legs, Ryker kicked wildly, finally pushing the older faerie off of her. She ran as fast as she could to the boulder and climbed to the top.

From her perch, she could see the entire meadow and the meadow could see her. She gave a whistle and pointed towards the bush with a sense of urgency. Climbing swiftly down the face of the rock, she ran back to the bush and waited as faeries gathered. With little hesitation, she pushed a branch aside exposing her siblings in their state of embarrassment and hurt. An audible gasp ran through the crowd as Ryker stood with a smile on her face. She waited for the laughter to spill from the mouths of the older faeries. When none came, she looked at them and urged them with her head.

Instead of laughter, Soma came from the crowd. She pushed her way through the gathering, and with a glare at Ryker, went into the bush. Gently the white-winged faerie helped the young wingless faeries stand and showed them how to hold their heads high. She led them out of the bush and into the daylight, surrounded by their family.

The crowd converged, hugging the tattered youth, making sure there was nothing more damaged or hurt with them. Several faeries flew away and came back with twigs and grass, using the same techniques Ryker had used to make her fake wings so that they could bandage and splint the damaged remains of her sibling's wings.

Ryker watched all this in a silent rage. Where were the laughter and the taunts? Where was the feeling of despair that followed her everywhere? Why were her siblings being coddled and she was left to stand on the sidelines, as always, ignored and rejected? She stomped off fuming. She would show them. They would see she was better than her siblings and she would fly. Finding her way to the oak tree, Ryker opened the little door and grabbed her newest set of wings. Putting the apparatus in place, the wingless faerie walked out the door and with a new determination, walked back to the boulder. This would prove her worth, she was sure of it. These wings she had made would show that she was a faerie, better than her siblings now were.

She climbed the boulder and stood, watching the other faeries coddling her brothers and sisters in the distance. The white-winged Soma stood in the throng, going from newly wingless faerie to newly wingless faerie. A hot rage filled Ryker and tears bubbled out of her eyes. Why hadn't they treated her as kindly? The girl stepped back from the edge and gave a running start. The wings caught the air and filled as if they were sails. Her feet came off of the boulder and Ryker soared. She caught the breeze and flapped, staying high above the flowers and the grass.

So blinded was the wingless faerie by her rage and want for revenge that she didn't hear the cry from the group or hear the wings beating as many took flight, racing towards her. She didn't feel the wings she had made splinter and fall apart around her. And she didn't feel the ground as it rose up to consume her.

The Sight-Stone

LESLIE D. SOULE

The year was 1917, and the sun shined down upon the yard and garden. Eleanor and Grace had the summer afternoon to themselves, and they spent it in the yard and in the fields nearby. Eleanor was sixteen and Grace was fourteen. Both had chestnut brown hair and eyes, and fierce curiosities. They wore their pretty white lace frocks, and hats with ribbons trailing down their backs. Eleanor was always at her books, and Grace hastened to pick flowers.

The two sisters spent many a happy afternoon together, playing in the garden or the creek just beyond it. A fact which brought Mrs. Evans much anxiety and distress. For a moment, Eleanor had set down her red, leather-bound tome, *Fairie Light* and gone to walk with her sister by the stream. All of a sudden, she spied something in the shallow water and plunged her hand in to get it, having waded out into the creek so that the hem of her dress was thoroughly soaked. She returned to dry land, carrying an ordinary river rock with a hold in the middle.

"Eleanor, Mother will be quite cross with you," admonished Grace, "getting your dress all wet and muddy just so you could chase after a rock!"

"Oh, but Grace, this is no simple rock," said Eleanor, holding the stone in both hands, reverently, as though it were a delicate baby bird. "This is a sight-stone. Jonathan Briar describes them in *Fairie Light*, if you look through one, you can see into the land of the fairies."

"Well what would you want to go and do that for?" asked Grace. "Fairies seem kind of boring. All they do is fly around and grant wishes to people."

"If you had one wish, from a genie, what would it be?"

Eleanor thought for a moment and then seized upon an idea. She gazed off dreamily and said, "I would wish to find a handsome prince, like in a fairy tale. He'd be charming and handsome."

Grace scrunched up her nose. "That may be all well and good for you, but I feel like your priorities are all messed up. I would wish to see the world."

Eleanor had found a rock with a hole in it, through which, if the legends were to be trusted, one could gaze and gain the second-sight, to see into the fairie realm that was typically invisible, hidden from mortal eyes.

She put the stone up to her eye and gazed through it. Looking through the sight-stone, she saw the glory and wonder of the fairie procession. Some of the fairies walked behind a tall female wearing a crown, while others rode dragonflies or rode upon mice like miniature steeds.

※ ※

"Oh, let us go and meet them!" She begged her sister to run off and find this procession, and both were equally excited at this prospect, but the girls had never dealt with fairies and did not know how tricksy they could be.

"Fairies grant wishes," said Eleanor. "The Fairie Queen may grant my wish to find a handsome prince, and yours, to see the world." Grace needed no further prodding, and the girls lifted themselves up off of the grass and took off running, pell-mell, down the hill and out to the field below. The fairies were quick little creatures. But eventually, they caught up. And then a strange feeling came over the girls, and they realized that either they were getting smaller or the fairies were getting bigger, or maybe both. Eventually, size became less of an issue, and then not an issue at all, as they stood at the same height as the fairies.

"Come and join us," the fairies cried, upon their approach.

"I am Queen Mab," said the fairie queen. She was beautiful, wearing a sparkling, white gown. She looked at Eleanor. "You wish for a handsome prince, and so you shall have one. My son, Helio Starlake, is looking for a bride."

A handsome man stepped out from behind her, and he was everything Eleanor could have ever hoped for.

"Oh, let us stop the procession and go back for Father's camera, to show him that the fairies exist!" The fairies consented, and Eleanor ran back, appearing minutes later with the camera in tow. The fairies had made Grace a crown of flowers, and four of them danced in front of her as Eleanor snapped the photo, and then set the camera on the ground. "We shall come back for it later."

Although a farmer walked into the field, he walked right by the fairie procession, and past Eleanor and Grace, as well. "It's like we're invisible," said Grace.

Day turned to night, and the girls saw small fires, like torches, off in the distance, and getting closer. "What are those?" asked Eleanor.

"Do not fear, my sweet bride," replied Helio. "Those are the torches of our enemies, and they are approaching. You see, I am the Prince of the Seelie Court. We like humans and generally treat them kindly." He pointed off into the distance. "Those, on the other hand, belong to the Unseelie Court."

The Unseelie Court attacked. The Seelie Court knew what to do, and the fairies all began to change form, one after another, into falcons who then took wing. The Unseelie Court had only themselves and melee weapons, no bows or arrows, or long-range weaponry. By this ruse, they were easily outdone. Helio attempted to grab Eleanor by the waist, to take to the air with her when he transformed. But Eleanor, as though possessed, shook him off and walked alone toward the members of the Unseelie Court.

They had no weapons upon them, and Eleanor saw none that she could borrow or steal, save for a small wooden bucket, standing by a tree. The fires of the Unseelie Court went out all at once, leaving the fading light of sunset. She looked away for a moment, and rather than the marching bodies of her enemies, she saw jewels strewn about the field of battle. She knew what had to be done, taking up the bucket and gathering the jewels with her sister, and then quickly overturning the bucket, so quickly that none of the jewels had time to run out, and they were trapped under the wooden bucket. Except for one ruby, which Grace had secretly kept in her hand.

The Seelie Court had time to return to their original forms and quickly return to the procession.

Helio landed and transformed. "Let us go, my darling."

They picked up the pace, and Eleanor grabbed her sister's arm. As she did so, the ruby flew out of Grace's hand and landed on the ground. There, it changed into an Unseelie, who threw Grace over his shoulder in a fireman's carry and ran off toward the overturned bucket.

"NO!" Eleanor ran in the direction of the retreating Unseelie Court, but she was much too slow. "What do we do now?"

She saw the Unseelie Court run in the opposite direction, and disappear into a portal that appeared in a gnarled old oak tree.

"Both courts come together for the Gathering and Masquerade Ball, in two weeks, where we all pledge to be civil and work out our differences."

The Seelie Court retreated into their own portal, at the base of a different oak.

※ ※

When Eleanor walked through the portal, the world she emerged into was unlike anything she'd ever seen. She stood at the gates of an enormous castle that glistened as though glitter were poured all over it. The very walls sparkled. The procession walked in, and Helio showed Eleanor the castle, which was massive, and eventually, to her own chamber.

Filled with anxiety and fear over the events of the day, Eleanor could not sleep, fearing for the safety of her sister. After all, the Unseelie Court was known for not being kind to humans, and Grace was very much human. She stayed awake in bed, and her betrothed came in to check on her, undoubtedly spying the candlelight that spread throughout the room and slipped beneath the floor.

"My darling," he said, "what keeps you up at this hour of the night? Does this palace not please you?"

And though she'd only just met Helio, she saw the pain evident in his facial expressions and felt that her heart should break from sympathy. "It's not that," she answered. "I merely worry about my sister, and how she will be treated by the Unseelie Court. These thoughts run rampant through my mind, depriving me of any ability to sleep."

Helio looked thoughtful for a moment and then crossed to the other side of the room, where sat a golden harp. "May I play for you?"

Eleanor nodded, but her heart was not in it. Then Helio began to play, his fingers lightly touching the harp strings. All of a sudden, as if by magic, the music soothed her soul. She yawned and stretched. "I'm so tired, all of a sudden."

"Listen to the music," said Helio, "and let it lull you into the sweetest sleep, free from worry, free from nightmares, and all other unpleasant things. I have in my fingers, the cure for insomnia, given to us by our blessed Queen, and to her from the former Queen, and on, through the ages, from the oldest of times. Hear my voice, my darling, and sleep. Listen to the music and to the sound of the breeze coming in through the window, cooling the night air. Listen to the sound of your own heart, and picture the clock winding backward slowly. Sleep." And soon enough, she was fast asleep.

Helio walked over, kissed his fiancé on the forehead, blew out the candle, and left her chamber 'til morning.

※ ※

She woke in the morning, but she'd dreamed of being in the world she'd always known, and it made for a strange, jarring juxtaposition. She realized that she knew so little about the world she now found herself in. *What, exactly, did the fairies do in the morning? And what did they eat?* She'd never given it much thought, and Jonathan Briar and his *Fairie Light* seemed to assume that they ate the same things that humans ate. But that didn't make a whole lot of sense, *how would they take down a pig to turn it into bacon? They might well steal the eggs of chickens or the milk of cows, but bacon? Or sausage?* At any rate, she supposed it didn't matter much. They survived somehow.

She journeyed downstairs, and the fairies had a tea party all set out for her, along with a feast of foods and confectionary treats. Instead of a teapot, they had an acorn with a teapot-spout, and instead of cups, they had little flowers in red and yellow. They had cakes and cookies and items she couldn't quite identify, dusted with powdered sugar, and Turkish Delight and bowls of fruits and nuts.

Eleanor sat down on a velvet-cushioned wooden chair and poured herself a cup of tea. She liked her tea with cream and sugar. The sugar, she found easily enough, although it was colored bright pink. As for the cream, it appeared all of its own, when she started stirring the tea. This would all take some getting used to.

She saw mushrooms in acorn baskets and acorns in mushroom baskets. She saw toast with rainbow-sprinkled butter, tiny strawberry shortcakes, little tarts, and cups of custard. A tiered platform held biscuits and scones. Sprigs of lavender in green glass vases decorated the table, and honey bees flew here and there, alighting upon them. The fairies had made the most adorable petit fours, as though the bakers among them were in competition with one another.

Many fairies were seated at the table, but Queen Mab was nowhere to be seen. At the small tables at the outer edge of the room, the child fairies sat and played at eating breakfast like they were adults. But they seemed more well-mannered than human children, by far. Eleanor made a mental note of all this. She'd have to write her own book on fairies, someday. The one she'd read said that fairies could not reproduce and that all children had to have been stolen from the human realm—but that couldn't be right.

Eleanor was nervous, at the prospect of seeing her sister again, and yet excited at the prospect of a Masquerade Ball. She'd never been to one before, but it was all so intriguing. The romance, the mystery, the masks, and gowns carefully sought out and chosen.

Queen Mab showed Eleanor to a huge room of the castle, where dresses hung from the branches of ivory trees, with golden leaves, and this vast faux forest ran off into the distance. There were *so* very many gowns.

Eleanor was absolutely delighted. *I could spend a month in this room, and not have tried them all on.*

Helio smiled, clasping his hands together. "Do you like it, my darling?"

"Oh, I love it!" she replied, giddy. She plucked a blue gown from the branches of a false tree, and ran toward a velvet curtain, to go and try it on. After a moment, she emerged, wearing the gown, and looked around for a mirror.

"Are there any mirrors here?" she asked.

"Of course," Helio replied. "But you have to call them to you. Simply look in the direction where you want to create one, and say, "Mirror, come forth!"

She did so, and a mirror materialized. "But you could have just asked me," said Helio. "I would have told you that you look incredible."

"Well, I wanted a second opinion!" Eleanor replied, running off in the direction of a new gown to try on.

When at last, Eleanor was done with the gowns, Helio showed her to the castle's library. "Now don't get lost," he cautioned. "This room only appears to be of fairly normal size. But looks can be deceiving. In truth, its shelves go on and on, as it contains a copy of every book ever written, in both the human and fairie realms. Also, it contains scrolls from the Library of Alexandria, which we saved from the fire, long ago." Eleanor's eyes lit up as she viewed this room, and then she pelted Helio with kisses.

"You seem to like it. This pleases me," he said stoically, politely. Part of Eleanor wished that the fairie prince would be a little more passionate and a little less polite. But nevertheless, she kept such thoughts to herself. But she must remember to tell Grace about this room!

All at once, she felt sorrowful. *Grace ... I wonder what's happened to her.* She turned to Helio. "Do you think I might someday be able to show my sister this room?" It was her informal way of bringing up the subject.

Helio looked sad. "Of course. And you will see your sister soon, at the Masquerade Ball. For now, take a look at this collection." He held out a green marble to her. "Should you need to find your way back, simply drop this marble, and it will teleport you back to this spot." He handed it to her. "Go. Explore."

She did so, marveling at all the books on the high, wooden shelves. She saw comfy armchairs, placed here and there.

As she wandered the aisles, she found the Fantasy section, her favorite. Only, this was no section as the shelves stretched on and on and on. She'd already lost sight of the beginning of the room. Every book she could imagine, lay here, in pristine condition, as though it were fresh off the printing press. Eleanor knew that this place was a wonder—outliving the destructive forces of the human world—fire, war, and numerous other record-destroying tragedies could not erase these tomes. Now, she had the rare opportunity to gain from this library—if she could only figure out how—the wisdom of the ages. She ran a finger along the spines.

"I have to relax," she told herself, plucking a book off of the shelf. The tome was made to look like dragon skin, and it shined with opalescence. The title, *The History of Dragons*, was imprinted on the cover, in curling, twisting lines of silver. *Worrying will do me no good, and it will not make the time go by any faster.* So she sat down in the armchair and started to read.

❧ ❧

At long last, the day of the Masquerade Ball had arrived.

"Sister," said Grace, dipping into a curtsy. She wore a black gown and matching mask, both covered in orange sequins.

Next to her, stood Helio's twin brother, Tenebrae. He wore a fine, tailored black suit. Eleanor wanted to strike out in a rage, but her sister and Tenebrae both belonged to the Unseelie Court, and if Grace had been poisoned by that philosophy, then who knew what sort of heinous acts would be on the table, if they fought.

A young boy came running up to Grace and stood at her side. Grace knelt down and kissed him on the cheek. "This is our son, Harael."

But it had only been two weeks that the sisters had been apart. Eleanor knew from her reading, what this meant. "That child is a changeling, whom you've kidnapped and taken from his parents."

Grace's eyes flashed with anger. Eleanor at once felt sorry for the child's parents, who undoubtedly would have found a shrieking goblin in their child's room, making a crazed, chaotic mess of things, instead of their darling boy, who looked to be about five years of age.

"You're just jealous of our handsome boy. Besides, what have humans ever done for you?"

"What about Mother and Father? They're waiting for us, probably worried sick."

"Oh Eleanor, you worry too much!"

"I do not!" Eleanor shrieked, stamping her foot on the floor. "Do you even know how much time has passed since we left? The stories all say that time passes slower in the faerie realm. We could have been gone ten years by now!"

Helio walked up to Eleanor and set a hand on her shoulder. Oh, how she hurt at the thought of having to leave her sweet prince. But perhaps he'd let her leave for just a little while, to visit the human realm again. If she and Grace could leave the fairies for just a day or two, and think about how far down the rabbit hole they'd fallen, and get their bearings, it would be all for the better.

As if sensing the conflict within her, Helio produced a crystal ball and held it aloft. In this crystal ball, he showed the girls their parents, frozen in time. "When you choose to go back, whenever that should be, it will be as if you've never been here. You may live a lifetime or five lifetimes, and can always go back, and your parents will be waiting for you, as will everyone else.

Next, Tenebrae stepped forward. "As for the child, he is a changeling ... that is true. But he was dying of influenza, clinging to life. There was a funeral. They'd given up their child for dead, and so a dying fairy chose to take its place and to be buried in the human realm. The magic ran out of him, and in the transformation of his body into stardust, the fairy magic could be released, curing any who wandered close to the grave. Small magic, but a sacrifice all the same ... and an ode to the beauty of life."

The girls began to visibly relax, as Eleanor turned to Helio, and embraced him, and Grace turned to Tenebrae and the child, embracing them.

"My dears," said Queen Mab, "You have made your wishes known to me. To Eleanor, I've given a handsome prince. For Grace, I have the sight-stone from your world, that will show her any place on Earth, and should she wish it, allow for travel there, as well." She handed the stone to Grace, who let a smile play upon the contours of her face.

"Thank you," she replied, accepting the stone.

"You are our guests here ... remember that you are not our prisoners. Should you wish to leave, you may. But should you wish to stay, you are always welcome."

The music started up, and there was much merriment and revelry, far into the night. The Seelie and Unseelie Courts together at last, and on friendly terms.

As for the girls, they did not know if they would stay here in the realm of fairies or for how long, or whether they would go back, but there was plenty of nighttime left, and a whole lifetime to figure out the details. So they danced with their fairie princes, throughout the night, and enjoyed the place that their sight-stone had brought them to.

The Perfect Escape

JESSICA SIMPKISS

I stood in the airport surrounded by the loudness and busyness that I was desperate to escape. I needed silence in my life, or maybe just the calming rhythmic crashing waves of the sea. If I closed my eyes tight enough, I could almost hear the sound of the waves itching at the sand over the noise of people scurrying down endless hallways with luggage clanking behind them, announcements over the loudspeakers, televisions with football games blaring at the bar. I had never been much for crowds, or gatherings, or people really.

"Your grandmother has passed," was all my mother's letter had said, which was more than she and I had said in years, not for any specific reason, we just weren't that close.

My grandmother had been the one to raise me. Her passing was overwhelming but not unexpected. As a little girl, we would lay in bed at night, and she would read me tales of mountains and glens on the way to an island at the end of the world where beasts of legend lived and swam in the sea. "One day," she always said, "one day, at the end, I'll find my way back there again, to the perfect escape, and swim away with a creature of the sea," and other funny things that grandmothers always said.

Her ashes had shown up on my doorstep one day in a simple box, I thought the package was a pair of pants I'd ordered online instead of a box ... inside a box, containing the only thing left of my grandmother. Tucked into the brown, rough packaging was a small book with a worn azure blue cover, the front page of which simply read *Creatures of the Sea and Other Tales*. I remembered the book well as one she'd read from, almost every night. The inscription on the second page held much more meaning. Even though the evidence of the tremors in her hand was apparent in her scribbles, I could see my grandmother in the words she'd left for me on the page.

"Here we are at the end, my dear. Follow the road painted with purple and yellow, find the perfect escape on the island at the end of the world. Take me back so that I can finally be set free and swim away with the creatures in the sea."

※ ※

I'd hopped on a plane to the distant land she'd whispered stories about in the comfort of my bed on rainy nights. When I looked out the window of the plane after we'd landed, I was hit with disappointed at the sight of cars, streets, buildings, and people instead of castles with moats and mythical creatures, like the pictures she'd painted in my little girl head. I still had a distance to go until I would find the place where I would let her go, where she could finally swim amongst the creatures of the sea. I pushed through customs and the crowds before jumping in a car and vanishing without a trace, just as she had always wanted to do.

The drive to the island at the end of the world would take all day and involve a ferry ride over troubled seas. I sped down single-lane roads, watching as the hillsides painted purple and gold sped by. Nothing but the cows and sheep left gambling on their baby feet. Stopping along the way to stretch my legs, walk in the wet grass, breathe in the smoky air around me, the tanging smell of a simple country life surrounded me.

Finally, as the sun gave way to the moon and my eyes could no longer follow the road or read the signs despite the English translation directly underneath the native tongue, I had reached the end, quite literally, as the road vanished, and a small cottage set out over the sea laid in front of me.

My feet crunched in the gravel as I walked down the drive toward the front of the house, giving way to a soft swish of the long grass against my tired legs, as I continued to the edge of the bluff to look down at the waves lapping at the jagged rockface below. It's peaceful, rhythmic cadence interrupted by footsteps crunching in the gravel behind me. The keeper, I presumed and made my way in his direction as the evening swallowed us whole.

"Are you Penelope then," his deep voice asked through the darkness, his face shrouded in the hood of his jacket, the only thing visible the hint of a tussled beard peeking out from behind the hood. The sky began to drizzle, its soft patter against the hood of my raincoat and the tip of my nose. The description of the rain was the only thing I'd managed to retain from the back cover of my airport bookstore purchase before tossing it in the trash on the way out. "You'll get used to it," the book had said, "and you'll miss it when you're gone."

"Penny," I answered, the absence of light against his face leaving me to feel like I was talking to a ghost.

"Penny," the ghost said, his words hanging in the dampness, stretched between us.

"The place is perfect," I finally said, cutting the awkward tension with my cracking voice.

"*An teicheadh ceart,*" he whispered.

"What's that?" I asked, confused by the words in his ancient tongue. Though I could not see his eyes, I felt them on me, snakes slithering against my skin, wrapping around me, my breath becoming shallow and weak.

"The perfect escape," he repeated, pointing to the front door, a tiny hand-carved wooden plaque hanging above it, displaying the cottage's name in words I could not read.

"Unbelievable," I laughed to myself. When I booked the last-minute trip, there had only been two or three cottages available of the seven that served this side of the island,

and I had somehow managed to book the one owning the name The Perfect Escape, unbeknown to me, not having been able to comprehend the language it was written in.

I started laughing, almost hysterically, my voice carrying out over the void of the cove below, creating an awkward few moments between myself and the keeper, as he watched me all but roll on the wet gravel. *It had been an actual place, all this time.* I'd always assumed they were just stories like every grandmother tells her grand-daughter. The hilarity of the situation was only curbed by the untimely realization that having lost my grandmother, I would never hear her stories again, never hear the real story of why she held this place so close to her heart.

"I'm sorry," I apologized to the ghost standing in front of me when I'd finally composed myself. "My grandmother used to tell me stories when I was a child, about a place called 'the perfect escape,' but I didn't realize it was real place until you said the name of the cottage."

There was silence for a moment, only the hiss of the hushed rain falling around us. Even the waves had quieted, having been mocked by my laughter.

"What stories would she tell you?" he asked, taking a step closer as his words hit me.

His question, or rather, his interest caught me off guard, and I fumbled for words to answer him. "She always talked about coming back, to finding 'the perfect escape,' and something about swimming in the sea."

"Did she ever make it back," he asked again, taking two steps closer this time.

I had been wrong about the air feeling silent before, I would have killed for the sound of the busy streets or noisy idle chatter, but instead, the rain hung in the air, and the waves ceased to roll. The world had stopped moving, it's perpetuation hanging on the keeper's words and my answer to them. The moon had risen just enough so that the ghost disappeared, and I could see the outline of his jaw under his hood, his thin lips curled tight hiding in a tussled brown beard. This exposure left me wanting more of him, as he stood just out of reach.

"No," I answered sadly. "Well, yes." And that was the truth. She'd never made it back on her own, but she was here now, in the only form of her that still existed. "She never made it back while she was alive, but I have her with me, in my suitcase. She'd asked me to bring her back and spread her ashes in the sea."

"Let me help you with your bags then," he offered, moving towards the trunk of my car.

We walked in silence toward the cottage, the rain having been released from its petrified state, dripping heavy from the clouds again. He unlocked the door and dangled the key in front of me, gently handing me the suitcase that held my grandmother. As he turned to leave, his hood slid slightly from his figure and in misty moonlight, I saw his eyes looking back at me; deep-set, sunken, ashen eyes, like the sky after a summer storm. Cloudy, but bright ... the worries of the day, gone and washed away. I looked at him looking at me, feeling the blood beginning to rush to my cheeks, becoming strangely aware of the heat of hunger under my skin. He was a stranger, I didn't even know his name, but I could not help but stare, something desperate in the way he looked at me begged me not to lose his eyes, like if I did, whatever it was between us, would be lost forever.

"If ye' like, there's a path to the beach just beyond the fence," he started, as he stepped out of the glow of the porch lantern and back into the shadow, his steel gray eyes still calling out to me from deep inside the darkness. "It's a bonny walk, and if it were me, that's where I'd want to be set free."

I watched this lips as the moved, and I heard the words, but I was barely listening. I had to keep reminding myself that this was a strange man in a strange land, even if it didn't feel that way. It was like there were two like magnets pulling between us, having just been flipped, desperate to connect with the other half.

"If you're lucky, ye' might see a selkie," he continued, perhaps feeling the pull urging him to take a step closer.

"A selkie?" I asked almost too tired to care.

"Aye, they're a special Scottish seal," he answered. "They frequent the beaches 'round here."

I wanted to grab his hood and tear it away from his face to finally get a good look at him. In my sleep-deprived, jet-lagged state, I was beginning to lose patience with the games the shadows were playing with me, keeping the whole of him just out of sight.

"Well … I'll let ye' be for the night, ye' must be tired from your travels." He turned to walk back up the driveway and disappeared into the moorland haze, the magnetic pull never completely disappearing, only weakening the farther it stretched.

❧ ❧

I slept like solid stone that night, heavy and motionless, weary from my travels, my mind too tired to think of things to dream about. I awoke the next morning to the sun creeping in under the curtains and the sound of sea birds calling. I searched the cabinets for coffee with my eyes still half closed, but whoever had stocked the cottage with bread and eggs and cheeses obviously did not share my affinity for the substance.

The air outside the cottage was crisp and brisk against my skin, the sun just beginning to sneak above the horizon, sending rays of ruby ginger flying across the sky. I passed the car at the end of the drive and kept walking down the road, hopeful that I would run into someone selling something that resembled coffee along the way. There had to be something in the nothing that defined the island, even the keeper had to eat.

At a bend in the road, I could see a building at the top of a rolling hill with several cars parked in front of it, giving it the outward appearance of being the something in the nothing I was looking for. I walked along the edge of the lonely road, looking down to the beach below as I moved, the little bit of white sand left uncovered by the sea glistening like a thousand tiny diamonds in the morning sun. The tops of tall rocks jutted out from underneath the water, dark and slippery, covered with green algae. Within the movement of the sea, I saw something swimming, playing in the waves, watching me watching it from above. *A dolphin perhaps,* I thought, as I looked through the waves of emerald and sea-glass green, feeling like it was begging me to join it for a swim out in the sea.

As I swung the door open, a loud, rancid bell chimed above my head, announcing my presence to the three people in the quaint coffee shop that doubled as an art gallery. All I cared about though was the thick smell of stale coffee in the air and the hiss of the steamer behind the counter, which played like music in my ears.

"Good morning to you Lass," a shrill women's voice called from behind the machine. "Ye' look like ye' could use a strong cup o' coffee."

"Please," I answered desperately, unwrapping the scarf from around my neck, despite it being June. The patrons pale and pasty skin made me wonder if it ever got warm here, if anyone ever had a chance to swim out beyond the sea.

The other two women had gone back to reading their papers as I meandered around the shop, looking at paintings on the walls and small trinkets for sale on the shelves. A quaint painting of a sad woman caught my eye from across the room, calling out to me to take a closer look. She was sitting on a rock surrounded by the angry sea crashing up around her, a group of seals crying shamelessly at her feet. *What had he called them the night before when I was too tired to care?* I would have to ask again.

"Here ye' are, dear," the shop owner interrupted as she held out a cup coffee to me, steam rising from the rim of the cup, pleading to be sipped.

"Thank you," I meant to whisper, but instead, what came out were garbled, tired words asking about what the keeper had called the seals when we had stood under the stars in the rain the night before.

"Aye, ye' mean the selkies," she purred, her words soft and sweet as she spoke, almost like the singing of a lullaby. "Tis but old folklore in these parts, of men and woman dressed as seals, swim among the sea, who come to shore to make love to human mates before sadly returning to the sea."

The coffee burned against my tongue, but it was her words in my ears that made me almost spit it back out.

"Dinnae laugh Lass, it's little lassies like you that the male selkies leave the safety of the sea to find. Watch yourself next to the shore," she warned, "if you see a man most irresistible, that'll be no man, but a creature of the sea come to pray on ye' and make ye' love him still, before turning to run back to the sea."

"Creatures of the sea," I whispered, the words echoing across the years of my life and ringing through the stories my grandmother told me every night. I looked at the painting and the sadness that plagued the women's eyes as she sat alone on the rocks. The figure itself was no one recognizable to me, but her eyes held a likeness I had seen before, a guise looking back at me throughout my childhood. It had faded in her eyes the older we both got, but it was always there, a longing for something lost but never to be forgotten.

"She is a female selkie," the shopkeeper added, seeing the perplexity spreading across my face. "Made to be a selkie wife to a human man who stole her selkie skin away." Her words gripped the hairs on my arms and neck as a shiver ran down my spine.

The two women sitting at the table opposite us burst into laughter, slapping their knees and table alike, their coffee cups wiggling and spilling into their saucers.

"Ach, Fiona, stop telling yer lanky tales to that poor lass. Let her coffee at least get to her gut before you start spinnin' your nonsense on her. Cannae ye' see the poor thing's still half asleep?"

Half asleep and paralyzed as the newspaper reading patrons in the corner continued to laugh at the shopkeeper, who scowled her brow and flapped her kitchen towel in their direction, as if they were unwelcomed pigeons on the porch needing to be shooed away.

"Dinnae listen to her lass," one patron warned, "but enjoy her coffee, best on th' island."

The storekeeper blushed and shook her head as she turned back to me. "Ach, no imagination, those too," she whispered, a wary smile developing on her face. "You let me ken if you need anythin' else."

"Maybe just one more cup ... to go," I whispered, trying not to be rude as the other two patrons continued to laugh and talk amongst themselves. It wasn't them, or the stories that had hastened my departure, I had only just become keenly aware of how much I wanted to take a shower once the coffee was flowing warm through my veins. I stopped at the outcropping overlooking the beach below before heading back to the cottage, but whatever had been playing in the sea was gone, and the only movement was left to the rolling of the waves.

I must have missed his knock while showering, warm water washing over me, thoughts of my grandmother's words mixed with those of the shopkeeper twirling in my mind like the soapy water snaking down the drain at my feet. Just inside the front door was a basket of what looked like gathered earth, with a note attached, labeling it peat—to burn in the stove—and next to it a grocery bag, with a small coffee maker and several bags of coffee. Normally, I would have cared more about the intrusion, the invasion of privacy—a strange man had let himself in while I was showering, but I could not discount his kindness and my need for coffee in the morning. I'd only wished I'd heard the knock and run, dripping wet, to answer the door, craving the feeling of his deep-set eyes wandering against my skin again.

The walk to the beach below the cottage was arduous, but worth the trouble; the wind didn't bite as much below the bluff. The air was calm and thick with salt. I found a flat rock to rest against and watched the ebb of the sea go in and out, my grandmother resting comfortably next to me.

I sat quietly for what felt like hours, listening to the sound of her voice in my memories being carried away by the wind. I tried to imagine her as a woman maybe my age, walking along the shore, skipping shells and wandering into the sea like she'd always told me she would do at the end. As long as I'd known her, she'd always had a cryptic way about her, never just coming right out to say what she meant, leaving me to decipher my own meaning from her convoluted words. I felt the tears dripping on my skin, triggered by the lost and squandered opportunities to have believed her and find the truth in the stories she'd told me. But then, they were just stories and in my mind, didn't warrant deeper thought. Now, all I wanted was to ask her what it all meant. What was she returning to and who was her creature of the sea?

I wiped the wetness from my skin when it felt like her memory and I were no longer alone on the beach. In the hours I'd spent sitting on the rocks, staring into the abyss stretched out in front of me, searching for the truth in the murky, muddled waters, I'd not seen another person, but now, I felt eyes on me, drinking me in, even though there was no one that I could see. The tide had receded, the shallow waters exposing what looked like a lonely castle rising up in the middle of the cove situated precariously atop an outcropping of rock which had most likely been deteriorated over time from the pounding of the sea against them. It looked familiar, and though I could not place it, it called to me, not by name, but in the crashing of the wave against the sand, rhythmically whispering all its ancient secrets to me.

I slipped out of my shoes and stepped into the warm sand, eager to feel the water, its chill stealing my breath as it ran across my skin. The tropical turquoise color had deceived me, I'd forgotten where I was for a moment, overlooking that the water would be so cold. But still, something called to me from the tiny castle perched atop the rock, as I scuttled closer toward it in the sand, wondering how far a distance it could be and if my body could make the swim.

What do I have to lose? I thought as I shed my clothes, knowing they would only drag me down once I was swimming in the sea. Left naked standing on the brisk, barren beach, I said goodbye to anything resembling a rational thought and dove into the water to swim to the tiny castle perched atop the rocks desperately calling out to me. *This is where you're supposed to be,* it had whispered in the waves against the sand. *Come find me, and I'll show you what love can really be.*

I didn't breathe as I swam, convinced it would only make me colder. It did not take long before I felt the pull of the current around me. Arms paddling as strong as they could, I was still no closer to the rocks and further from the beach than I could believe. My lungs began to burn for air as the rest of my body began to freeze. The current pulled against me, memories of my grandmother and her stories of the creatures of the sea flooded me. I fought against the current as it pulled at me, tugging me in a million different directions, not wanting to be a runaway to this foreign land who ended up freezing in the fucking sea.

I had not thought much about death, not intending to have died when I dove into the water, I'd only wanted a closer look at the tiny castle that had been calling out to me. I wasn't sure what I'd expected death to be, but it was sweeter than any story had ever led me to think it to be. The tickle of a kiss against my lips, so gentle I almost missed it, an excitement I had forgotten, a warm sensation itching against my skin and a pounding upon my chest.

The thick sea air burned inside my lungs more so than the salty sea, the mixture of the air pushing in and the sea swimming out creating a jarring feeling of both pain and relief. I realized I wasn't dead when I could feel the coarse, warm sand against my skin and dancing through my hair, when I could see the rings of the sun dancing just outside my hallucinating eyes.

Who had been here to see me drowning in the sea? Who had seen me, and whispered that this is where I was supposed to be? Surely a fisherman must have seen me, I thought, blinded by the powerful sun, my hands clamoring out in front of me for the truth of who he or she might be.

There was nothing in the void around me, nothing in the nothingness surrounding me, but as my arm recoiled empty and all alone, something took my hand, and in the nothingness, I found the truth, swimming with me in the sea.

His hand was warm and wet, rubbery like a kitchen glove, but soft and loving like a mother's touch. I blinked my eyes, trying to blink the glare away, but with the sun hanging close behind him, he was nothing but the outline of a figure, holding my trust tightly in his hands. My throat was hoarse when I tried to talk even though there were no words to thank him, so I let him stay in the shadow, my body weakened by the fight, shivering in the summer sun with a stranger holding me tight.

"Are you alright?" he whispered, his lips creeping closer to my ear.

"Who are you? How'd you know I'd be here?" I asked, still searching for the shadow in the light.

"I've been waiting for you, you were always supposed to be here" he answered, as we fell into a wistful kiss.

His lips were soft, tentative at first, while he let his wiry whiskers rub against my lips. There was an electricity between us; a charge, a spark, a catch … something passed between us as our lips touched and I remember then how much I'd always loved the sea.

I told myself it was all a dream—the brains mechanism to save me the humiliating pain of having just let a stranger steal an unsought kiss and the pending attempts for more, trying to instill a bit of grace in almost drowning. The man was probably a fishmonger looking for an easy score and took his chance on a vulnerable girl he'd just fished from the sea, not possible to be the fairy tale creature knelt before me.

Just as quickly as I'd found them, I'd lost them, his lips, as his shadow disappeared from blurry view. I wanted to cry, like he'd died, having lost the feeling of true love forever. My body shivered and convulsed involuntarily, the hypothermia I was sure was setting in, my fingers and toes and the tip of my nose tingling with numbness while the rest of my body burned, the spark he lit with a kiss already beginning to grow.

I was in his arms, pressed against his pounding chest, as he bounded up the cliff to the cottage above us. The peat was already burning warmly in the stove when he set me in front of it and against the warmed tile floor, still half-naked, dressed in sand and smelling of the sea.

He knelt behind me, the heat from his body warming me. I could feel him, hear his quiet breathing, sense his eyes hugging me. Once warmed and with wits about me, I gathered that my company was still that of a stranger, and pulled the blanket he'd wrapped around my shoulders closer to my skin, leaving less to the imagination.

"I should go," he whispered when he saw my movement, making him play the role of an unwelcome voyeur.

I spun around, but he'd already turned to go, his back to me. "Don't go," I gulped, trying to keep the most pathetic two words in the English language from slipping past my parting lips, but instead of the thud of a door slamming behind him as he fled, my words stopped him in his tracks. He turned slightly, exposing just enough of his profile for me to see his thick, rough beard covering his square jaw and hiding the thin lips that he had just pressed against me.

"Are you sure?" he asked, a statue in the sun's reflection.

"Yes," I answered calmly, unsure of what it was about this stranger that made me want him so.

He stood tall, towering above me before he knelt to join me on the warmed stone floor. His stormy eyes met mine and the world melted, like butter in a pan, leaving only he and me in solid form. His hair was the color of good whiskey and his beard a shade or two darker. His skin was worn, tanned by the sun, and glistened in the light. I had never seen a man so beautiful, never seen a man as beautiful as he, staring back at me with eyes that screamed words no language could ever hope to be.

What had the shopkeeper said, "take care along the shore? Not a man that'd be," she'd whispered while making coffee, "come to make love to lonely women before sadly returning to the sea." *Am I the lonely woman? And the man that knelt in front of me, not really a man, but a creature of the sea, one like my grandmother had always claimed to be?* I struggled as the fabric of my reality gave way to the tremendous weight of the truth that had been laid on top of it. I didn't know the questions to ask to get the answers that I needed, so I just looked into the haze of his smoky eyes, ready to listen to everything he had to say.

"I've been waiting for you," he whispered as he took my hand in his, lips planting yet another kiss, his touch leaving lustful blisters burning everywhere they went. "I thought you'd never come."

His voice was windy and deep like the sea crashing roughly against the rocks. I touched his face, my fingers winding through his fluid whiskey hair, his love for me, thick and hanging in the air.

"How'd you know I'd find you here?" I asked as he moved closer to me, the magnets pulling us closer and closer, our bodies shaking under the pressure of the fight to stay apart just a little while longer.

"The stories said you would," he breathed, his lips and eyes holding close to mine. "Stories of a woman slipping willingly into the sea."

"Tell me what your stories say, about me, the woman you found dying in the sea," I sang, to which he answered with another kiss, this time wild and remiss.

He told the story with his hands, swaying on my skin, "the stories say she'll come one day, and slip gladly into the sea." Had I missed this tale in the azure colored book just a room away that my grandmother had left to me? I remembered stories of kelpies, tangies, and banshees but nothing of creatures of the sea come to make love to lowly little women like me.

"I've called to you for a thousand years and would call a thousand more," he whispered. "My calls crying out to you, in whispers rolling with the sea."

"How does the story end," I asked. "After you find the woman that might be me?"

A smile danced across his face, and his eyes cried that there was nothing might about me.

"It's never-ending," his lips explained, "when we slip back into the sea."

His hand caressed the skin against my cheek, and I felt the catch, the spark, the charge again ... the electricity ignited, and I decided to live a thousand years with this creature of the sea, however real or imaginary, uncaring if the later should he come to be, as long as the thought of him touching me still made me weak in the knees.

"Stay with me," I begged, "before returning to the sea. Lay with me," I whispered, "for the next thousand years, and then a thousand more."

He loved me deep and rough, a thousand years of yearning finally being set free. He came to me this way, every day and every night, to lay with me until it was time for him to return back to the sea. The sand in the bed and his salty smell on my sheets my only assurance of his existence, of the man that had waited a thousand years for me to find him and willingly slip into the sea.

"Are you ready," he asked, his ashen eyes delving deep inside me.

His coat was cold and wet, unnatural to my touch. "Here," he whispered, placing it around my shoulders. "Keep it tight, and you'll be warm, and the coldness of the sea will cease to be."

He turned to me, before diving back into the sea, the cold water lapping at our feet. I held my grandmother in my arms, wondering if this was where she'd always wanted me to be.

"Just breath and listen to the sea," he whispered. "Breath and be with me."

He kissed me quick and then disappeared, the thought of ever having loved before him a sheer impossibility, as it had only ever lived out here with him, between the waves crashing into the sea.

I inched my way deeper until the water was above my knees. I tore the paper box and let my grandmother drip into the water rough and wild all around me, finally escaping with her creatures of the sea. I slipped inside the coat hanging against my skin before I swam into the sea, listening to all the things my grandmother had bestowed and left to me; the secrets to finding 'the perfect escape' and the keeper, my creature of the sea, and me, the woman she'd set free.

The Night Garden

DAWSON HOLLOWAY

The wind seldom blew across the Night Garden. It seldom ever even paid it any mind—a world swaddled in darkness so much that not even a fleeting spark of starlight could be seen—nothing ever turned an eye to the Garden. That was just how Antonio's father liked it.

Under his father's guise, Antonio had been watching over the Night Garden for years, his father had handed him his sickle when he had taken his first breaths in manhood, now his jet-black hair was beginning to run in gray waves above his ears, his cheeks caving further into the bone every day. But, Antonio did his job well. The Night Garden was black with shadows—the ground, the air, the skies, the trees, all consumed with darkness, except for one place.

"The moon is allowed," his father reminded him every single day, "but only the moon may be your friend. No other may offer its light to the Night Garden."

Antonio never lit a torch, never produced a spark. The Night Garden bathed in blackness. The moon was his only friend. His father always watched from his bedroom window, the moon gleaming against his staunch, unmoving wrinkled face, his thin pursed lips. Antonio would come home from the Garden, make him a salad, a sandwich, anything that didn't require a fire to cook, and tucked him into bed every night. His father was much too old to move his arms and legs with the frivolity of his long-past youth.

Only then would Antonio take to his chambers, only to wake when the darkness summoned him next to the fields.

But, there was one instance where he couldn't do it.

Something was pounding against Antonio's skull. Something that pried his eyes open, something that perked his ears. There was a presence that tickled his spine, that constricted his throat, that spun his brain around its finger. There was nothing else in the world that Antonio knew besides his father, the moon, and the darkness. None of them would find any value in depriving Antonio of his rest. There was something else calling to Antonio, and he and it agreed that he needed to discover what it was.

Antonio slipped out of his bed, letting his feet barely patter against the floor as he slunk out of his room, sneaking past his father's door, the shadows following his every step. He didn't bother putting on shoes as he swung the door open—they were too clunky, too loud. He closed himself out and took off running into the night.

It had been years since Antonio felt the grass between his toes. It was softer than he remembered, it tickled his toes just as it had in his youth. In the midst of the darkness, as he toiled in the fields, Antonio could never help but neglect that it was there. Whatever blades caught a glint of the moonlight overhead only ever glinted silver for an instant before the darkness reclaimed it. Antonio had never once seen the green that his fields would have claimed in other worlds. All he knew was darkness. That was just the way his father liked it.

Antonio reached the top of the bridge crossing the river, his favorite place in the Night Garden, ever since he was a boy, to calm his racing mind. The grass, the trees, they all tried so hard to grasp the fleeting moonlight with such little success, but the water of the river caught it so effortlessly in its glossy surface. The churning waters distorted the moon's image but captured its luminescence all the same. The river shared the light with what trees and shrubs nested near it, creating a monochrome paradise along its banks. It was truly the beauty of the Night Garden.

The light, almost absent wind brushed across Antonio's hair, the water gushed and babbled beneath his feet as they dangled from the bridge, his toes almost dipping in. Antonio closed his eyes and listened to the Garden. When he opened them, they were facing the moon.

"What is it like to have so much light?" Antonio asked.

The moon was silent. The breeze whispered, but Antonio couldn't hear what it was saying.

"I envy you," Antonio smiled.

He heard a voice from over his shoulder, "It is best not to envy a friend."

Antonio whirled around, half-expecting to meet the face of his father, but he saw instead the masquerade of a short, frail thing, skin the texture of wood.

"You must be Antonio," it said. "Keeper of the Night Garden. I was wanting to speak with you."

"I am he," said Antonio. "Who are you?"

The figure sat down next to him, letting the moonlight gloss over his face, his arms, his clothing, his legs, now dangling off the bridge, as well. He had pointed ears, a long crooked nose, beady black eyes—blacker than Antonio's own.

"My name is Mackey," he said. "I am an elf."

"I've seen nothing like you before—"

"No one," Mackey corrected Antonio. The elf smiled. "I travel from world to world ... I am not much more than a tourist."

Antonio eyed Mackey. The elf sounded well-rehearsed as he spoke, somewhere in the backburners of his wooden head must have been a script to answer the questions that most commonly came his way. Mackey was already prepared to tell Antonio where he'd been; the Frozen lands, the Aurora, the Red-Dark Seas, perhaps. Antonio's father had tried to tell him stories of such places—stories that others had told him once—but they were merely interludes in passing conversations. Neither Antonio nor his father had ever seen such worlds. Neither of them had seen colors, besides the black of the night and the white of the moon. Neither of them were interested in learning. There was too much work to be done in the Night Garden.

"Why?" asked Antonio.

Mackey curled his eyebrow, surprised. "Why do I travel?"

"Yes," Antonio said. "Why bother?"

Mackey chuckled. "It isn't a bother," he said. "I enjoy it."

Antonio's face was no less puzzled. "Why?"

Mackey shook his head, growing a smile, the corners of his lips curled in pity. "I am a gardener, as well. There are many different flowers and plants around the world ... I like to collect my favorites."

"Then why did you come to the Night Garden?"

"Because it's beautiful," Mackey told him, turning his eyes to the river. "I have seen places that try so hard to be beautiful with so many different flowers and arrangements and shapes. They are beautiful, truly ... I have seen worlds that I once could never have imagined. But, I have seen so many that I am no longer surprised by them."

Antonio was looking at the river now, too.

"This beauty is different to me, though," Mackey said. "Your Night Garden is a world running deep with shadows, but there is this pocket of tranquility. It is beautiful in a way that I have forgotten beauty can exist."

Antonio smiled. "It is all I have ever known ..." he said, a pinch of mourning echoing in his voice.

"So, you have never seen the flowers of other worlds?" Mackey asked in shock. "Not even Night Brushes?"

Antonio shook his head.

Mackey scoffed and produced a satchel from his leather sack. He unwrapped it, pulling out a plant. It was small but had many budding branches, flowers at their heads. The flowers felt unnatural to Antonio, though. They defied what light the moon offered to them, staying the purest black as Mackey kept his hands around them.

"Would you like one?"

"Oh, yes," Antonio said. "Father would love that!"

"Come with me, then," Mackey said. "We'll plant it by the river bank."

The two of them dashed to the shore, Mackey producing a spade, digging a hole, stationing the Night Brushes in their new home. Antonio smiled, they were perfect.

"What else do you have?" asked Antonio.

Mackey did not hesitate to rifle through his bag for his different satchels, producing another flower, the Masquerade; another flower, the Dark Quill; another flower, the Obscura; all fitting beautifully with the Night Garden. Mackey and Antonio planted several of each, and then more; Umbrage Lotuses were released into the water, seeds for Usher Trees were planted on the heights of the bank. A rainbow of monochrome lived across the riverbank now. Antonio smiled as Mackey took little saplings and samples of the Night Garden's flora for himself.

"There is one more flower that I want to show you," Mackey said. "But, you may not like it."

Antonio's eyes glossed over what flowers the two of them had planted together, the Night Garden had never reveled in such beauty before. "I'm sure I'll love it," he said.

Mackey smiled as he pulled a final satchel form his sack. He unraveled the bag, letting loose a bulb. The elf unfolded his bark-coated hands from it, and the bulb slowly unraveled. A purple light began to seep from its petals—each petal was marked with the dim white stars of the universe, a purple nebula stretching across the flower's opening face. In its heart—in the stamen and the style—was a white that burned with the hotness of a sun. Antonio screamed, jolting back and falling on his hands.

Mackey grinned. "Do you like it?"

Antonio shook his head. "Father wouldn't—"

"Do *you* like it?" Mackey asked.

'No other but the moon may illuminate this field,' Antonio's head hurt with the voice of his father, but his eyes were caught by the purple of the nebula. The cloudy dust slowly moved along the petals with the weight of the universe pushing it, a rainbow of violet hues was suspended in the blackness of the flower. The white,

heavenly glow from the heart was so powerful. For the first time, Antonio could see the brown of the elf's wooden hand, hints of green on the grayscale grass, the peach color of his own skin. His eyes were transfixed onto the flower.

"I ... I—"

"This is called a Celestial," Mackey told him. "It is one of my favorite flowers. I think it is perfect for the Night Garden. I have more in here ..."

Antonio's eyes darted away from the flower as he struggled to spit out, "No! *Stop!*"

It was too late.

Mackey produced another Celestial. Its petals unfolded in a blue-green light, instead of a Nebula stretching across its surface, there was a galaxy. The flower had another blazing white heart, only it was surrounded by the oranges, blues, greens, and yellows of stardust. Antonio's eyes were transfixed again. The colors of the flower echoed through the gray Night Garden, they echoed through Antonio's head.

The galaxy Celestial was beautiful.

"Go back to the bridge," Mackey told him. "You grow so much darkness, yet you know nothing of the beauty of the night. Let me show it to you."

Antonio was silent, stone-still. His head still echoed with the cold voice of his father, *'No other but the moon may illuminate this field,'* but the cosmic beauty of the Celestials had captured his mind. Antonio slowly took to his feet, he slowly took to the bridge. He let his feet dangle from the edge, dipping into the water, as he watched Mackey plant the flowers.

Every Celestial had the same blazing white core, but from there, each one was different. One had a black hole siphoning the infinite light, one had a red plane orbiting around it. One was only painted with stars, one was painted with massive galaxies colliding into the most beautiful mesh of colors. Each one that Mackey rooted into the ground illuminated the grass a little more, the pinks and oranges and greens of the trees, the blue of the water.

The Night Garden   Dawson Holloway

The colors of the Night Garden, for the first time, began to shimmer and melt together. For the first time, the true colors of the night could be seen.

The colors bounced off of Antonio's brown eyes, his beige shirt, his blue jeans, the red lips lining his open-hanging mouth. They bounded off of his pearly teeth as they formed into a smile.

Mackey was next to him again. Antonio looked up at him, eyes filled with wonder. Mackey smiled and snapped his fingers, the Celestials folded back into their bulbs. The river knew nothing but gray once more, the moon was its only friend.

Antonio was baffled now, his eyes trembling. "What happened?"

"That's the beauty of the Celestials," Mackey said. "They allow the new and the old to exist in the same place. Snap your fingers."

Antonio did, the flowers unfolded once more, washing the darkness again with the colors of the universe.

"The Night Garden was beautiful on its own," Mackey said. "However, I think it is only fair for it to know many kinds of beauty."

Antonio smiled graciously. Mackey nodded back, slinging his leather sack over his arm.

"What is this?!" echoed a roar from over their shoulders.

Both of them whirled around, only to see Antonio's father trudging towards the Night Garden, cane in hand, the light of the cosmos glowing against the red inferno blazing across his enraged face.

Antonio snapped his fingers, the Garden folded back into the moonlight.

"What was that light?" Antonio's father roared. "What was that color?"

His father was at the bridge now, Antonio began to shake and sputter, "N-n-no!"

Antonio's father thrust his cane into his son's chest. "I told you that the moon could be your only light!" he shouted. "Night in and night out … only the moon can touch my fields!"

"Father!"

"You've failed me!" Antonio's father told him. "You've failed my Night Garden!"

Mackey's fingers snapped, and the Garden blazed in a fire of color that burned against Antonio and his father alike, washing through them in a mesh.

"Your gardens?" Mackey spat. "Antonio is their keeper … the gardens are his!"

Antonio's father lifted his cane and whacked it against the elf's head. Mackey peered over at Antonio, cradling the wound, and disappeared in a flash of white. The Garden went dark again.

"For thousands of years, my garden looked like this!" the old man shouted. "For thousands of years, our family preserved this beauty! How dare you let yourself derail from this tradition. How *dare* you let an elf manipulate you? He understands nothing of the beauty of darkness!"

Antonio thought about taking another step back, shaking more, pleading 'Father!' again, but all he could do was clench his fists, his face curling into anger.

"Because Mackey was right!" Antonio shouted. "This is my Garden! The beauty we have worked so hard to preserve is still here … it is in front of us! But, now there is something new! Something I want to keep!" The different colors flashed across Antonio's mind, the shapes of the cosmic bodies etched across the Celestials. "I want the colors of the night in my garden, too. And I want you to admire it for what it is."

His father's face untwisted as Antonio's soured more. The fires of rage between them petered out. They were left in the glow of the moon, the gush of the river, and its dimly lit banks.

"I want you to love what is here," Antonio said. "All of it. What's yours and what's mine."

His father was silent. For a moment, Antonio was, too.

"Snap your fingers, Father," Antonio said. "See what the Night Garden has to offer."

Antonio's father hesitated for a second, but a light click rang from his side after the silence.

The Night Garden blazed in an inferno of color all at once. The Celestials roaring their colors louder now than before, their hearts burning brighter. The colors of the night burned through again, against the grass, against the brush, the trees, the water, the bridge, Antonio, his father.

"Do you think it is beautiful?" asked Antonio.

His father let the slightest smile escape him as the colors of the Night Garden burned against his watering eyes.

The Mermaid

of

Puget Sound

JJ SIEMS

Olivia was a twelve-year-old girl who was prone to flights of fancy; almost always preferring to inhabit the lands she saw in her head. It was a blessing and a curse. A small crooked smile would curl upon her face as she told herself and others fantastical stories, but this same delight also betrayed her as it made Olivia the target of cruel school-yard bullies and parents who didn't have the patience to indulge their daughter's fantasies. Which is why it was so peculiar that on one unusually dry Seattle evening she couldn't think of a story to offer her mother in explanation when she arrived at her home dripping wet with no recollection of the afternoon's events.

Her mother looked at her bewildered, "What happened to you, Olivia?" The little girl thought for a moment. *What had happened to me?* After a momentary pause she looked up at her mother, "I don't remember."

Her mother scowled, dragged her upstairs, and plopped her into a warm bath. "Olivia, I've told you this so many times! You know I don't appreciate lying. It doesn't matter to me if you went swimming or ran through sprinklers, just be honest about it when I ask you a question. I will not have my daughter grow up to be a liar," she said, vigorously scrubbing her daughter.

Olivia sat in the water, quietly trying to figure out where she had been and what she had been doing. Still blank. Her mother sighed, defeated. "What are these things in your hair?" She pulled out little twigs and leaves that seemed to have made a nest in the little girl's tresses. Olivia picked up the twigs and stared back at her mother with a vacant expression. Her mother wasn't sure if she should be worried or not—perhaps Olivia was just going through a bout of depression?

Her mother pulled her out of the tub and began drying her off with a towel. Olivia whimpered as the towel yanked her hair and scalp. Finally satisfied with her daughter's level of cleanliness, she left the bathroom and instructed Olivia to get dressed and come down to dinner.

Olivia stood naked on the bathroom rug wiggling her toes and watching as the fibers molded to the shape of her feet. She felt hazy, as though the fog rolling in from the Sound—as it did almost every day—was drizzling in her head. She heard her mother shouting her name from downstairs. Olivia scratched her head, watching as another twig cascaded down to her feet, before finally changing and heading down to join her family for dinner.

"Olivia, what's this I hear about you coming home soaked?" her father asked in between mouthfuls of bloody steak.

The little girl shrugged, the disoriented feeling hadn't abated at all.

"Because, I don't know if you're aware, but on the news today they said that three children drowned. You shouldn't have been out swimming by yourself," he replied sternly.

Olivia flicked her fork around her plate but didn't eat anything. "Maybe they deserved it," she said quietly, her eyes never leaving her plate.

Olivia's mother dropped her fork; the sound of the screeching tongs against the dinner plate hurt Olivia's teeth. "Olivia!" her mother cried out while her father looked on, dumbfounded, "What kind of thing is that to say?"

"I don't know what I meant. I don't feel well, I need to sleep. May I be excused?" Olivia finally said.

Her parents looked at each other with concern but ultimately continued eating their steaks. "Yes dear, so long as we're clear that we don't want you out and about without telling us where you'll be. And definitely no swimming by yourself!"

Olivia nodded and trudged upstairs to her room.

※ ※

That night she tossed and turned, her foggy mind disturbed by unsettling dreams. She could see herself floating under the murky waters of what appeared to be the bay. Her pale skin was blue, and locks of hair floated all around her as though fingers had weaved through it, scattering her hair in all directions. A mass of leaves and tree branches floated above her head, entwining with the floating hair. Her eyes were open but lifeless, staring ahead into the deep water. Her arms reached out, to what, she couldn't see.

The perfect stillness of the vision was interrupted by the voice of another girl whispering, "We're really friends now. Friends forever."

Olivia shot up in her bed. The first light filtering in from her window gave the room an eerie, azure glow. The tree branches outside her window gently waved in the breeze beckoning her with their tendril fingers. The movement was hypnotic, peaceful in the otherwise stillness of daybreak. Her trance was interrupted by the flitting of a hummingbird hovering outside, seemingly looking in. Olivia lay back down, staring straight up trying to form pictures in the popcorn ceiling. Olivia still couldn't remember what happened yesterday. *I must have hit my head really hard!* she thought.

❦ ❦

Her mother came crashing into her room an hour later with her usual morning hectics. "Olivia, time to get up, I didn't have time to make your lunch, you need to go do that now. I'll be in meetings all day, so if you still aren't feeling well, call your father to pick you up."

Groggily, Olivia got to her feet and dressed. When she brushed her hair, more twigs fell out.

She stepped out onto the porch and shut the door behind her. The air was crisp and sweet as a breeze blew through flowers and honeysuckle freshly watered by the rain. There were patches of sun and blue sky amidst gray rain clouds—the norm for Seattle at this time of year. Despite the nice weather and the liberating freedom of being outside, Olivia still felt that odd sense of confusion. She started her walk to school, lost in thought about nothing in particular. Her neighborhood was dotted by ancient drooping trees, weathered moss-covered stones, and tall bushes. Lake Union with its houseboats and pristine water was on one side, and Washington Park with its arboretum and exotic flora was on the other. It was anything if not scenic.

"Where did you go? You didn't come back!" A frantic young girl's voice broke the silence.

Olivia stopped, startled. She looked around. No one was there. She paused a moment, straining to hear. Nothing except the usual sounds of birds singing, rain drizzling, and cars passing. As soon as she resumed walking, she heard it again, this time louder. The voice was wailing.

"You said you wanted to be my friend. You said you would come back! Please come back my Olivia! Please come back."

Olivia looked around tentatively and said, "Who and where are you? I don't see you."

"Our spot by the water, Olivia. Come now, hurry!" The voice was urgent and sad.

Olivia paused, trying to decide if she was hearing things or not. First strange dreams, now haunting voices. What was happening to her?

Suddenly, a very real voice dripping with hatred interrupted her thoughts. "You! It's you! Yesterday, our friends followed you to the water ... Now, they're ... they're gone. But you're still here. What did you do to them?" On the corner ahead of her, a group of kids from Olivia's school—tormentors all of them—looked on like a pack of wolves sizing up its prey.

She breathed hard, tears filling her eyes. *Why do they always pick on me? Why do they care about me at all, I'm no one,* she thought in anguish.

Olivia sucked in air and cried out, "I don't know what happened! I don't remember anything about yesterday. I don't know what you're talking about!"

"Liar!" the kids screamed as they charged her.

Olivia turned hard and began running toward the lake. The group of bloodthirsty bullies laughed maliciously as they gained on her. The quiet neighborhood with the stoic trees, green lawns, and water-worn houses, now felt like a horror movie with Olivia, the victim.

There was an inlet of water fenced off from the 520 freeway entrance that was shielded by a mini marshland with a thick blanket of trees. Olivia waded through the murky marsh and hid behind a tree that seemed to be rising out of the water. She watched as the group of tormentors scattered in both directions on the shore trying to figure out where she went.

Olivia silently waited for them to give up and wondered how long she had before the school would call her parents.

※ ※

On the opposite side of the inlet, houseboats eerily rose from the mists of the water; small dinghies on their docks bubbled up and down in the choppy waves.

"Olivia, my Olivia, I'm here. Hurry!"

The ghost voice startled her once again, this time it was close, she could hear its sharp pitched sadness. When she was satisfied that the other kids were gone, she tentatively made her way back to land.

She followed the shore past a grove of trees, a few hundred feet away from any of the houseboats. She heard a splashing beyond a large rock jutting out of the shallows. Olivia ran over, eager to see to whom the voice belonged. As she rounded the rocks a sense of both wonder and dread came over her. Before her, skulking in the shallows was the oddest looking creature.

A mermaid.

A girl.

But it wasn't beautiful as she had always assumed a mermaid would be. Its tail, flopping about on the water's surface, was a yellow-green and looked more lizard-like than she would have expected. There was a clear distinction where the fish part stopped, and the human part began, but a few yellow-green scales were interspersed on the pink flesh of the torso. The mermaid's neck and sides of her jaw were also covered in the scales, making her look as though she wore a turtleneck. Its dirty brown hair looked oddly similar to Olivia's—disheveled and full of twigs and leaves. The mermaid's eyes were like a cat's, the pupil thin and long like a line. The creature smiled excitedly, showing off rows of sharp teeth when it saw Olivia approach. It gasped for air, like it was a struggle to breathe, as it spoke.

"Olivia! My Olivia! You have returned! What took you so long my lovely girl?" The mermaid looked to her eagerly. It steadied its torso on its elbows, careful to keep the rest of its body submerged in the shallow shore water.

Olivia's confusion grew. She was intrigued and couldn't tear her eyes away. Against her better judgment, she stepped closer to the creature, getting a good look at its monstrous form, "What are you talking about? What are you?"

The mermaid let out a little howl—like a beaten dog. Its eyes flashed both anger and sadness. Tears trickled down its cheek.

"Oh Olivia, you've forgotten! My friend, you've forgotten what you must do so that we can be together."

"Are you the reason why I can't remember anything? Why I feel so strange?" Olivia asked.

It rose onto its hands, the mermaid's head now level with Olivia's eyes, "Yes, my friend. It's okay that you don't remember, that sometimes happens. I told you to go home and say goodbye, but I should have had you go straight there. No matter, you're here now, and that's what counts," the mermaid girl gave Olivia a sharp smile. "You found me here yesterday, we talked for hours. You told me about how lonely you are. About how the other children won't play with you. I told you then, it is the same for me. I'm the only one like me here. Meeting you filled me with such joy, I want you to come live with me, forever. We can be friends, forever." The mermaid girl slinked back into the water.

"Come live with you?"

"Yes! You said yesterday that you wished you could be a mermaid, like me," its face dropped, and the mermaid rasped, "Have you changed your mind? Please tell me you haven't, my Olivia."

Still in a woozy trance, Olivia plopped down in the water; not caring that she was ruining her clothes and her backpack full of school papers and notebooks.

The mermaid gave her a nervous grin.

She stared at the mermaid in delighted wonder, thinking about all the stories she had heard, all the movies she had seen. It must be so wonderful to be such a creature, carefree in the water not having to worry about school or overbearing mothers or mean children who call her a freak and chase her—

"Oh ... now I remember why I came here yesterday," Olivia replied sadly. She had never understood why she was so hated by the other kids at school. Olivia spent all of her time at recess reading or telling herself faerie stories by an old tree at the furthest edge of the school property. Why did that make her a target?

"Yes, my Olivia, yes. I heard what those children said to you. They don't understand you, no one here does. Not like I do, my Olivia. Please tell me you haven't changed your mind."

She shook her head vigorously, "No, no I haven't changed my mind. I want to be a mermaid like you. What do I have to do?"

The mermaid's voice grew nervous and high pitched. Animatedly, it gasped as it spoke. "We've already started the process. Take my hands, my Olivia, it will be easier to show you." The mermaid reached out to her, its hands almost the same size as her own with webbed, clammy, snake-like fingers that beckoned.

Suddenly, a vision overtook Olivia. She saw herself, skin pale reflecting blue light as she floated underwater with lifeless eyes and reaching arms. It was what she had seen in her dream. It had really happened yesterday. The vision was like a movie playing in her mind. She saw the three bullies chase her down to the water. She saw herself hiding behind the rock. Then the mermaid appeared, and they talked and laughed and sang. The mermaid grew serious and asked if she would stay with her so they could be friends forever. They held hands, and the mermaid pulled her under the waves and kept her there until her breath ended.

Olivia screamed and pulled her hand back, "You, you drowned me?" she cried.

The mermaid stood on her hands again, her tail flopping, her voice desperate, "Yes, I'm so sorry my Olivia, it is so hard to understand. But look Olivia! Look what I have done for you!" The mermaid grasped Olivia's hands again, and the movie in her mind continued.

In the vision, she could see herself rising from the water, a pale disoriented corpse. The mermaid looked on, smiling, as Olivia stepped back onto the shore and trudged home like a zombie. The mermaid then began singing, and a few minutes later the bullies returned, in a dream-like trance following the heavenly voice. When they reached the inlet, the mermaid smiled for them, and laughed, and sang. The bullies, enamored by her charms, joined her in the water. When their guard was down, the girlish face the mermaid employed, distorted to that of a terrifying demon—her eyes grew large, black, and murderous as she bared rows of sharp teeth. Olivia's bullies screamed, but it was too late. They each disappeared under the waves, the mermaid thrashing about hungrily after them.

"The three kids who drowned, that was you? You killed them too? What kind of monster are you? You're not any kind of mermaid I want to be!" Olivia screamed through her tears.

The mermaid's eyes twitched. Her voice was low and menacing, "I did this for you. They hurt you! I hurt them back. They are of no matter now. Forget about them, forget about your world where no one cares or understands."

Whimpering, Olivia replied, "Even if I wanted to be a mermaid, how could I? I'm dead!"

"Oh, Olivia, no! This was part of the process, it was just delayed. For you to be like me, you have to leave your world. But it's not as simple as just that. There is magic to be done, my girl! There is a plant, it is a magical plant, but I cannot get to it. You see this plant is hidden and can only be found on land. You must bring it here so that I may enchant it with a spell, and then you must eat it. Then, and only then, will you be able to stay with me forever. You were supposed to do that yesterday, but you seem to have forgotten, I think that sometimes happens when one is dead. That is okay though, there is still time."

Tears streamed down Olivia's face. She couldn't believe she had been so lonely and so foolish as to trust such a creature. The other kids from school were horrible. They called her a freak, they locked her in basements, they hit her with the rage that stems from the hurt within their own horrible lives, but this creature had murdered her.

"What do you mean there's still time? I don't want this. You said I could be a mermaid, you didn't say I would have to die first. I've changed my mind. I can't stay with you forever, you killed me. You're not my friend!" she wailed.

The mermaid's eyes dilated in anger. It showed its sharp fangs and screamed, "You can't change your mind now! I put a spell on you to keep you moving. If you don't eat the plant now, your already dead body will rot and decay. You only have a few days before that happens." The mermaid tried to soften her voice, "You've come this far, why not stay with me? We are friends Olivia, and we'll have all the time in the world to talk and play and laugh and sing. All you have to do is bring me the plant."

Ever since yesterday's incident, Olivia had felt blank, vacant. It was as though she didn't care about what happened to her, didn't care about the world around her, she just existed. After she collected herself, that horrible feeling of indifference returned. She no longer had a life, no longer had a choice. Olivia wiped the tears from her face and stood up, water pouring out of her soaked clothes. "Where is it, what does it look like?"

The mermaid sighed in relief, "Yes, good! You must bring me a stinging nettle plant. They grow near creeks and are chains of green leaves with jagged edges. Find the stinging nettle and bring it to me, I will use my power to make you a mermaid and then we will be friends forever, my Olivia."

Olivia blinked and nodded.

❧ ❧

Olivia was stewing as she headed out on her quest. She was incredulous that she had allowed herself to be tricked but mostly sad that the one chance she had for a normal life was now gone. The hazy fog clouded her mind once more and her hatred of the mermaid creature dissipated as she resigned herself to her fate. She may be dead, but at least she wouldn't fully die.

The only creek she knew of nearby was in Washington Park by the arboretum. The park itself was huge and fairly foreboding for a little girl out by herself. It was full of giant drooping trees, trees that seemingly grew out of waterways, flowers, and berries of all varieties, and hopefully, somewhere amongst all the exotic plants would be the stinging nettle.

After trudging along absently for an hour and a quarter, she found the creek hidden behind a grove of trees near the picnic area. As it was the middle of a weekday, she was alone, no children played. The patches of blue sky had turned to gray like it did almost every day, and the chill in the air picked up. Olivia looked along the banks of the creek. It was dotted with little green sprouts but not what she was looking for. She followed the little bubbling stream for a couple hundred feet before she had a distinct feeling that she was being watched. She looked around but saw nothing but hummingbirds flitting around.

Suddenly, Olivia heard a strange whisper in her ear. "I know what you're looking for, but you won't find it without my help."

She jumped. "Who's there?" She saw no one, but it seemed as though the hummingbirds were swarming. She'd never seen so many in one place.

"You can't give her the nettle. You can't become like her."

"Where are you? I can't see you. Come out, tell me what you know about her," Olivia shouted into the trees.

One of the hummingbirds flew right at her. Olivia blinked and put her hands over her face defensively, but the bird had stopped short. She opened her eyes, and there before her was no hummingbird; it was unmistakably a faerie. She couldn't tell if it was a boy or a girl, but whatever it was, it looked like a small, winged elf cloaked in ragged leaves.

"That creature is evil, little girl. You mustn't become one of them," the faerie spoke authoritatively for a being that looked her age, no more than twelve.

After all that she had seen, the fact that she was speaking face to face with a faerie didn't seem all that unusual. "I don't have a choice. I'm dead already. She tricked me."

"If you're dead already, then one might argue the noble thing to do would be to end this quest."

"What do you mean?"

The faerie's wings buzzed. "Don't you see, little girl? The mermaid tricks children to meet their watery ends. You are not the first to come here seeking the nettle. Don't give it to her, don't become one of them."

"You're saying I should just let myself die?"

"What if we said that you didn't have to die? What if we could help you? If we agreed to help you, would you choose not to be a mermaid?"

Olivia nodded, "I hate her. She killed me. She said she was my friend, she's a liar."

"Excellent, follow me, little girl," the faerie slowly started to fly away. It led her deeper into the park. She couldn't believe that a park in the midst of the city, could contain such magical creatures. The faerie stopped in front of a large tree and faced her.

"This is a Rowan tree. It has been used for centuries to ward off witches and demons," the faerie picked a strange white berry from the tree's branches. "This berry, if consumed by you, will restore your life. Everything for you will be as it was before. However, for a demon, for that mermaid, it is poisonous."

"You want me to kill the mermaid?" Olivia asked, intrigued.

The faerie nodded.

"Why though? Why are you helping me? Why do you want her dead?"

The faerie looked at her sadly and began to fly away.

"She used to be one of us. But now our sister is nothing but a monster."

Olivia grasped the berry protectively. She reached into the tree and picked several more. *I could just eat this and go home, it will all be over*, she thought. But the white-hot rage she felt as she thought of her vision, her own death, made that thought a temporary one.

❧ ❧

The mermaid was waiting in the same position she had been when Olivia left, crouching nervously in the shallows, her tail submerged. She brightened, showing her sharp teeth when she saw Olivia approaching.

Olivia's hands held tightly to the berries in her pocket as she thought of her plan.

"My Olivia, you are back. Did you bring the nettles? Quickly, my Olivia, bring them to me."

Olivia forced a smile and produced some green leaves from her pocket. "Here are the nettles!"

The mermaid grabbed for the leaves hungrily. Her nails were sharp and claw-like. As she cradled the leaves floating delicately on the water between her hands, she spoke strange words, and her eyes glowed. Before she finished, Olivia interjected, "I also brought some special berries mermai—wait, I don't even know your name."

The mermaid looked up in slight annoyance, "Melusine. What berries?"

"Melusine, that's a pretty name. Oh, the berries are from a tree near my house. They're delicious I eat them all the time. I thought I'd have them one last time before I become a mermaid and can only eat ... whatever it is you eat."

Melusine showed her fangs in an awkward smile. "Let me have one then, are they sweet?" she asked eagerly.

Olivia popped a berry into her mouth in relief. "Oh yes, very sweet. Here you go."

The mermaid opened its mouth. Olivia shuddered as she popped the berry in between the rows of sharp teeth. She could hear the berry squish as Melusine devoured it greedily, her face filled with chilling contentment. She turned back to the nettles and continued the strange words. Olivia's mind raced as nothing appeared to be happening. Melusine stood once again on her hands and beamed, "The nettles are ready my Olivia. Come my most dear friend, all you have to do is eat—" her voice trailed off, and her face fell.

Olivia felt as though a burning poison was pulsing through her veins. Normally she'd scream out in pain, but the sensation was warm and comforting—and alive. Her breath returned, as did the color in her cheeks. "My Olivia, what ... what have you done?"

Suddenly, Melusine howled, and Olivia watched as the mermaid began to dry up. The skin on her hands and face wrinkled up like prunes, and the scales on her neck and tail dried up like a snakeskin left in the sun. The look on the mermaid's face was one of agony and despair, but Olivia felt nothing but satisfaction as the monster met its end.

❧ ❧

Yesterday she had arrived home soaking wet. Today she looked as though she was returning from battle. "Olivia! Where have you been? We've been worried sick. The school called, you were cutting? I can't even believe it! I am so disappointed in you! Well, where were you, what were you doing?" her mother shrieked.

"No more kids are going to drown mysteriously around here. I killed the mermaid," Olivia said with gritty pride.

"Olivia! What did I tell you about lying?"

The Fairy Maze

ANDREA J. HARGROVE

Enter the fairy maze.

Somewhere in that limitless labyrinth, hidden behind a bush or under a bench or inside a log, a fat green caterpillar spins its cocoon. After it transforms, it heals the first human she touches, curing him or her of all aches and ailments. If you find the cocoon, you can wait there, hands spread above the wrapped silk threads. You can ensure that you are the first.

No one knows where or when the maze will appear—not even me, and I live inside it. Really, that's why I never know. Neither time nor place in the human world means anything to me. The only thing that matters is that I tend the maze and the caterpillars until one is ready to undergo metamorphosis, and then I hide it carefully and secretly. I tend the humans, too.

Last time the maze opened in an almost-forgotten mountain pass. The only who entered the maze before the way closed was an old lumberjack whose hand had been crushed by a tree. He'd needed very little from me except companionship during his vigil.

This time, the maze opened behind the king's castle, and I sensed that there would be companions aplenty. I, myself, fluttered between the tall hedges that bordered the maze, peeking out and waiting there with my heart beating fast and my wings beating faster. I waited as the maze called to them.

They always described it like a tingle in the back of their minds, urging them to drop whatever they were doing and come at once. Most never did. They had laundry to scrub or a roof to patch and no time to waste on foolish impulses or the half-baked notion that the wise old village woman had once told them a story that started with just such a tingle. So the dirt washed from their laundry, the rain stayed out of their houses, and they remained unchanged.

This time, six humans entered—six who found no meaning in laundry or roofs. They all stirred at the same call, and when they obeyed it, they all saw the same flowering hedge with the arched entrance dripping with budding vines.

A boy ducked in first, glancing this way and that, and tugging a wool cap low over his head. Aware of the others close behind him, he ducked around a bend in the hedges to listen.

An old man in his bedclothes entered soon after, sniffing the air and rubbing fallen petals between his crooked fingers. "I've heard stories," he murmured to himself. Then he jumped at a strange clacking and scurried to the same hiding place as the boy.

The two collided with a yelp, startling the two next arrivals. A woman dozed in a rickety wooden chair with a much-patched quilt draped over her lap. The chair had two thin wheels on either side, which clattered over the hard path as the woman's daughter pushed it forward. The maze had not called the daughter, but she obeyed her mother's impromptu request for an outing and was still allowed entry. Now that she realized where she was, and recalled the half-forgotten stories of childhood, she clenched her fists tightly around the chair handles and resolved that she would be the one to find the cocoon on her mother's behalf.

After them, a thin man with a twisted foot hobbled in, gritting his teeth with every step. He supported himself with a knobby stick that bent under his weight. Another stick rapped against his shoe from behind, and he grunted.

The owner of the second stick halted, and her free hand flew to her mouth. "I'm so sorry, but I'm just getting used to this." She listened carefully, waiting for him to move to the side before entering the rest of the way into the maze. "I'm blind," she explained unnecessarily. The milky white eyes surrounded by puckered scars spoke for themselves, as did the long cane that she swung back and forth in front of her, tapping the ground and any obstacles in her path. "Although, I thought I saw a flowered archway for a moment."

He shakily waved away her apology as he struggled to regain some sense of composure. Then he realized that she couldn't see the gesture. "Never mind that, and I believe you did see the same archway as us."

"It's a shame I can't paint it."

The man's face brightened as much as it could through his distress. "I thought I recognized you. You're one of the artists who live in the castle."

"I was until the princes decided they no longer liked my paintings. Then they blinded me and turned me out."

"I understand," the man replied. "I danced in the castle until the princes decided they no longer liked my dancing. Then they crippled me and turned me out."

The mother and the daughter listened carefully to the two as they spoke, and even the old man and the boy began to creep closer until the artist innocently asked the dancer, "Are you here to search for the cocoon?" The others drew back when she said it, all realizing what she seemed to have forgotten.

The dancer couldn't escape the question. He found himself backed against one of the hedges near the exit, but he wasn't about to leave without touching his moth. "Yes, I suppose we all are."

Her face glowed with pleasure. "Perhaps we can search together. You can lean on me as we walk, and you can guide me at the same time."

He shook his head reflexively, again forgetting for a moment that it meant nothing to her. "What would we do if we found it? How would we decide who got to touch it?"

"We could let the moth decide for itself. We could both sit near it … or all. I think I hear others. Then we would simply wait and see who it chose. It's better than not being able to find the cocoon at all. It's better than no one being chosen."

The boy laughed at them and surveyed the three paths away from the maze entry. "I'm the best hunter in the land. I'll do better without being slowed down by the two of you. And when I find it, I'll be the only one there, not one of six."

"One of five," the daughter corrected. "I'm only here for my mother." He skipped away regardless, taking the narrowest path in the hopes that difficulty would conceal the prize, and the daughter threw up her hands in exasperation. "We don't need him or his tracking skills. I'm sure the most deserving will find the cocoon, and that certainly isn't him."

Hearing her words, the artist asked, "So you accept my proposal?"

"I don't know. I was talking to my mother." She sighed, realizing her mother was still sleeping, and asked the old man, "What do you think?"

Scrawny shoulders plunged down as he grumbled, "No one cares what I think."

"I care."

Surprised, he dropped the last of the flower petals that he'd been holding. "I think … I think that in a maze this vast, we have little hope of finding one small cocoon on our own. If all of our eyes work together, we can travel faster. Oh." He glanced at the artist.

"I suppose I could work on my own. My eyes won't help your cause."

"Nonsense," the old man replied, though he couldn't say why. The dancer jumped in to supply a reason for them.

"The maze brought us together, and you've now brought us together. We can't just abandon each other." He pushed himself away from the hedge and dusted the needles off his back. Then he linked the dancer's arm through his own. "Shall we?" he asked the others.

The daughter looked between them all and between the paths as well. "I wish I knew what my mother would want, but she's asleep more often than not." She took a deep breath. "I suppose I'll have to trust in the way she raised me. Yes, I believe we should work together, and that makes all of us. Which way should we start?"

"Straightest seems best," the artist decided, to which they all agreed.

Then they set out together—limping, clacking, and shuffling, but walking straight.

🌿 🌿

After fleeing from his competition, the boy began to look for signs of the low trees favored by most of the kingdom's moths and to search around them for cocoons. He only found one of these trees, as I try to vary both the plant and animal life throughout the maze. The hedges are the same all the way through, but I like to see different shapes and colors standing out amidst all the greenery. I even move around statues, gazebos, and fountains when the mood strikes me.

At this moment, the moth tree was next to a goldfish pond I'd just added, and the reflection of the flowering tree in the still water had a pleasant effect that the boy was not in the right frame of mind to appreciate. He ignored both water and flowers as he pawed through the tree and then crowed in triumph when he spotted a cocoon. And then he found another and another. The tree concealed twelve in all, and the boy paled for a moment.

I bit my lip to keep back a squeak of pleasure. Like all fairies, I do love to see the humans momentarily baffled every now and then, and I'd thought the moth tree a fine touch when I planted it.

It could be any of them, he thought to himself. I listened in to his thoughts as a matter of course. It may seem intrusive to humans, but to fairies, it is all perfectly natural and acceptable behavior. *They all look the same. I suppose I could sit here and wait for them all. After all, the moths won't all break out at the exact same moment. But imagine if I had to chase them all at once!*

He began to pace, kicking at the ground and uprooting clumps of grass. When pebbles came up with the earth, he toed them into the pond, scattering the fish.

But what if this isn't the only tree? I can't watch all of them. That means I need to figure out which one of the cocoons is different. He compared the size, shape, color, and curve of each silken treasure chest and found them identical. *They're the same. Exactly the same. I'd bet that a magical cocoon looks different than regular ones somehow. If none of these stand out from each other, that means that none of them are right.*

He was right, of course. Now, what will he do with this information? I wondered. I decided to test that question by steering him back toward the others. Having already noted his preferences, I darkened the path that I wanted him to take and gave it plenty of thorns to grab at his clothes. Occasionally, I blocked a path that I didn't want him to take, but I let him make most of his own decisions.

It took half a day before he found the others again thanks to all the twists and turns, but they hadn't progressed far in that time. He swaggered past them, chin high. "You haven't found it yet?" he jeered. "Well, it's back that way by a pond, nowhere close to emerging. I'm going to find food before I settle in for the wait."

"You shouldn't leave the maze," the artist advised. "I don't think you'll be able to get back in."

He almost hung his head, but he soon regained himself and deserted them once more, though I decided to stay with them. *That should keep them out of the way,* he decided, *and so the prize will be mine.*

※ ※

The band of travelers rested by the goldfish pond after searching the moth tree and realizing the boy's trick. "'Best hunter in the land' he said," the daughter scoffed, dangling her bare feet in the water and enjoying the nibble of fish on her toes.

"He did find moths," the artist pointed out, tracing one pear-shaped cocoon with her fingertips.

"I'd still wager he sent us here on purpose to waste our time." As she spoke, she kept one eye on her mother, still asleep, and the other on the old man, now sitting propped up against the tree and wheezing heavily. He shifted once to rub at the spot where the skinny trunk was digging into his back and then collapsed against it again. *How much time does he have to waste?*

"Six months," I could have answered, "but he's in no danger inside the maze."

I alighted in a branch that just brushed the top of his head and leaned down to breathe on him. The dewdrop breath of a fairy always refreshes weary travelers, and the old man suddenly straightened and drew in a lungful of air with an ease that surprised him.

"I think I could keep going for a while," the old man said.

"In another minute," the dancer begged. *Maybe not at all. How long should I make them wait for me? It might be best if I went home.*

That wouldn't do at all. The point of the maze wasn't for anyone to give up. They had to work out the prize amongst themselves. It didn't always end happily, but I always had hope that it could, so I sprang into action, ready to give them the opportunity and see what they made of it.

I zipped to a nearby part of the maze, plucked a seed from an unobtrusive white flower, and carried it to the side of the pond. As the daughter dried her dripping feet she'd pulled from the pond, I planted the seed beside her cast off shoes and gave it a little puff. The flower sprang up instantly as I hid again.

The daughter finally reached for her shoes and froze with a frown when she spotted the flower. Then she slowly donned her footwear, all the while glancing between her mother and the dancer. "I found something that may ease your pain," she said at last, "and allow you to continue." She pointed at the little flower. "Chew the roots of this plant, and that should help you for a few hours."

He scooted closer to the pond and farther from the tree with its decoy moths. "You know I'm not much competition to you," he said, not sure how to phrase his thoughts inoffensively.

"I'm not trying to poison you. I swear the plant is safe unless they are different in this maze than they are out in the rest of the world." She took the initiative and dug up the plant for him, broke off a few strands of the roots, and washed them in the pond.

The dancer accepted the limp, dripping strands with trembling hands and then popped them in his mouth. He began to chew slowly, screwing up his face at the bitterness that followed. "Thank you," he said regardless. "Are you a physician?"

"Yes, as my mother was before me before age made her ill and forgetful. She was even the royal physician until—"

"Until the Princes cast her aside?"

The daughter pushed herself to her feet and adjusted her mother's blanket. "No, when I saw the cruelty of the princes, I convinced her to retire peacefully, before they could turn against her. Why would they trust a healer who couldn't even heal herself? She couldn't heal my father, either. He died of plague last year."

"You were wise to take her away." The dancer allowed the artist to help him to his feet as soon as the roots began to take effect. The old man refused an offer of assistance from the daughter as he took to his feet, leaning against the moth tree instead.

They continued forward as a band, trying one path then another for three long and quiet days before coming to a garden. Whenever they got hungry, tables full of food appeared around a corner. Whenever they grew tired, they found mats and blankets spread out on the ground. The mother woke up a few times, but mostly she muttered things about fairies and went back to sleep.

She was just rousing again on the morning of the third day as the party reached a vast garden spilling over with life. Birds and rabbits and other small creatures frolicked through the flower beds and between the bushes. Moths and butterflies, too, teemed around the garden, giving the humans pause.

The old man lowered himself onto a stone bench, bewildered by the throngs of winged insects. *If we find any cocoons, will they be false leads, too? How will we ever know?*

The others by and large wondered the same thing, though the artist buried her nose in flower after flower, soaking in their perfume until she ran into a marble statue of a deer. The dancer apologized for not stopping her in time, but the artist waved that idea away, as she'd been pulling away from him this way and that. Now, she stopped to run her hands along the deer's back all the way to the tip of his tail. "I can feel every hair," she marveled. Then she returned to stroke the head from the grainy antlers to the wrinkled, leathery nose. "I never knew how much you could do with stone, but this is incredible workmanship. I could never paint with this much detail."

"Fairy craftsmen use magic," the dancer said with a smile. "Plus, they live longer than we humans do and have had longer to perfect their art. I'm sure they could've out-danced me on my best days, too."

"I think I want to try this—sculpting, I mean—whenever we leave. Even if the moth doesn't pick me, it may give me something to look forward to. As much as I want to see the beauty of the world, as much as that means to me, maybe I can still feel it and create it in some other way. Don't you think?" she added when he said nothing.

"I think I hope the moth picks you," he confessed. "If you want to see so badly, I don't think sculpting can replace that."

"Of course not. Nothing could. But maybe I don't need my sight to still be myself."

"It's not the same," the dancer insisted.

"I know." She pet one almost velvet ear as she spoke and made her way down its neck and the dancer mirrored her movements.

"I've thought about these things, too ... about ways to hold onto my identity without actually doing the thing I love. I've thought about becoming a dancing instructor, for one thing, but I know that I would never feel as free as I did when dancing myself."

Their hands, each on their side of the deer, met the lump of the buck's sturdy shoulders, and they both naturally turned in toward the chest. "Then I hope the moth picks you," the artist countered. Their hands touched and continued down together until their fingers encountered one soft imperfection.

Just under the curve of the chest, where it started in toward the stomach, a pear-shaped cocoon gave slightly at their touch. They jumped back with a gasp, and the artist cried, "We found it!"

The old man and the daughter rushed over, though the dancer warned, "Let's not get carried away." He did have to add, "Though I did feel something. A tingle in the back of my mind, like when the maze first called me."

"And I saw something, just for a second, in my mind, as I did at the archway."

The old man and the daughter touched the cocoon as well, locating it between the front two legs of the life-sized deer statue right where the artist pointed. "I feel nothing," the daughter admitted, "but then again, this maze wasn't meant for me." She returned to her mother's side to rouse her and to steer her chair next to the statue. The old man knelt beside it in a daze, and the mother sat in a similar state as her daughter guided her hand.

The mother touched the cocoon and truly jolted awake for the first time since her arrival. Finding herself face to face with the old man, she gasped out, "My King!"

The others all pulled back a step, and the artist timidly asked, "Are you the King? But I thought ... I thought he ..." She blushed and turned away.

"You thought I was mad? Once I heard a fairy flute and tried to follow it down a path. My wife stopped me, and then she called me mad. She used it as an excuse to lock me away in a tower so that she could rule in my stead, and our sons after her death."

"I would have known the truth," the mother said, "if I had been allowed to see you."

Beard sagging to his thin chest, the King sighed with the futility of the idea. "I'm sure you would have, faithful physician, but I saw no one but my wife and sons from then until the maze called to me. Somehow, I chanced upon a secret passage that lead me to safety."

"It must've been the fairies."

"Yes, I hoped ..." He wiped a tear from one blue eye. "I hoped that they were trying to right the wrongs of their kin. You see, my sons dare not kill me themselves for the same reason my wife did not. It would cast grave doubt on their claim to the throne and weaken the loyalty of the people. However, they found an evil fairy to place a curse on me. The fairy said that I would die on my next birthday."

"How long do you have?" the daughter asked gently.

"Six months from today I turn sixty years old, and I am starting to feel my age. When that passage opened, and I found this maze, I wondered if the cocoon of legend would be enough to break the curse."

The mother belatedly bowed in her chair as much as she could, folding herself over her old quilt. "Then I hereby withdraw from the quest. I never would have asked my daughter to bring me here if I had known who else was searching for it."

"Mother!" the daughter exclaimed, not sure if she cared who else had been searching for it.

"No, my daughter, I could not take this opportunity in the King's place."

"If you truly want to leave, I'll take you away, but I beg you to reconsider."

"Besides," the King added, "hearing your story, and the stories of these two here ..." He gestured at the artist and the dancer, "I'm not sure I should take the opportunity in place of my subjects. It's my job to protect my people, and I've been doing a poor job of it for the last twenty years." His mind turned back along the endless, unvarying wheel of days. Sometimes he'd tried screaming for help, but he supposed those sounds only confirmed what the Queen had been saying. The mother tried to protest, but the King continued, "Either way, my people still believe me mad. Whether or not I survive the curse, I still need to fight that rumor."

The daughter considered this and said, "Given how the princes behave, I'm sure they'd be happy to say that you're sane, given half the chance. Don't you think so?" she asked her mother.

The mother agreed. "Despite my age and my recent troubles, I am still a respected physician. The court all know me, and since I left of my own accord, there was no cloud over my departure. If you will permit me to return to the castle with you, I will declare you fit and whole. I will make them listen."

The King drew himself up awkwardly and began to smooth his beard. "Thank you, my friend, if you will permit me to call you that, and perhaps you and your daughter would be willing to help me with one more detail." He cleared his throat. "You see, whether or not I survive the curse, I am bound to die one day, as we all do. As matters stand, that would still leave the line of succession uncertain, since I plan to disinherit my sons and arrest the lot of them as soon as I can. They are clearly unfit to rule."

"If you say so, my King," she murmured politely while the three younger folks nodded enthusiastically.

"Perhaps the two of you would do me the honor of joining the royal household. As my new Queen," he clarified, catching her blank stare, "and as my daughter, respectively."

"My King, I am not worthy—"

"Nonsense. You are a wise and skilled woman who's dedicated her life to this kingdom, and clearly, you've passed on all your best traits to your daughter. If I had a child half as loyal to me as your daughter is to you, I would be a happy man."

It took some time for the proposal to sink in, and even longer for mother and daughter to whisper together about their futures and the future of their kingdom. Then, at last, the mother replied, "We would be honored, and we will also do all we can to help you break the curse if the moth does not touch you here."

"But now," the daughter said, returning to the matter at hand, "we need to decide who will touch the moth first. Do we all still agree that we should let it decide for itself?"

There was no other way, and they all knew it, so they all agreed sadly, each wishing for another to be healed. When they all settled in their half-circle around the front of the deer, the King said, "But I believe one of us is still missing—lost somewhere in the bushes."

"Him?" the daughter asked, repulsed. "He wasn't part of our agreement."

"He is one of our subjects." The daughter had no rebuttal, so the king called out, "Boy!"

They all joined him in calling out at intervals until the daughter eventually realized, "We don't know his name. We don't even know each other's names."

With a tired, wrinkled smile, her mother said, "Sometimes it's hard enough to remember that you're my daughter, much less what I called you. Besides, I don't think names matter so much in here. Boy!" she croaked out.

That was the last call before the boy came tramping out of the maze. "What is it?" he demanded, haggard and frustrated from his futile hunt.

The king pointed at the deer statue. "Here is the cocoon. We have all decided to wait together for the moth to emerge, and we would like you to join us."

With bright saucer eyes, the boy scurried over and clutched at the cocoon. He nearly snatched it from its hiding place and ran off with it, but feeling the weight of the others' gazes, he released it and found a place in the semi-circle, which parted for him. "I don't understand."

Despite the ample room on either side of him, he sat tense, with his shoulders drawn in to avoid any accidental contact.

"You were called here, too," the daughter pointed out from her seat on the far stone bench, well away from the deer.

Her mother added, "You deserve the same opportunity as the rest of us. There's no fairer way to decide."

"But I ... but it's not fair. You don't even know what's wrong with me."

"We don't need to know."

"Yes, you do," he insisted, ripping the cap from his head. "It's this." They didn't understand at first until he parted his shaggy hair, matted down from the cap, to reveal a red "T" shape burned into his skin.

"It's what?" the artist asked the dancer softly.

"He was branded a thief."

The boy's head bobbed up and down. "I poached a rabbit, but the game warden, he said because I was only fifteen, he'd let me off easy, without even cutting anything off, but he gave me this mark. That's why I'm here. To get rid of some stupid mark on my head. It doesn't even hurt anymore. I'm not crippled or blind. I just wanted to start over."

Tentatively, unused to physical contact himself and dealing with a particularly skittish child, the King rested a hand on the boy's shoulder. The boy didn't shrug it off; he was too confused by the touch. "You may get that chance," the king said, "one way or another."

"It's moving!" the dancer exclaimed suddenly. The group fell into a respectful hush, all staring intently at the rocking protrusion beneath the deer—even the daughter, who was too far away to see, and the artist, to whom the distance made no difference.

They sat still, waiting several long minutes as the rocking produced a tear at the fat end of the cocoon and after that, a pair of scurrying legs clawed at the open air, followed by the rest of the body. The head and antennae popped free, along with its torso and the rest of its legs, and of course, its wings. They took time to shape themselves, but eventually, they unfurled proudly, displaying four eye-like dots set in orange and brown.

"This is it," the dancer whispered to the woman whose hand tightly squeezed his own.

The moth broke free from the statue and flapped in a circle as if weighing its choices. *Get on with it*, the boy thought, squeezing his eyes shut. Then something tickled the top of his head, and he had to keep himself from swatting it. A collective gasp went up from the others and then a sigh. The hand on his shoulder gave a little squeeze and then slipped away.

"Well done," the old man said, as if he had anything to do with it.

Was it me? The boy's mind hadn't quite caught up with the facts yet.

"Well, that's that," the dancer said. "It chose the boy."

That encouraged the boy to open his eyes and feel the top of his head. Something light brushed against his fingers and fluttered away, and the tiniest of weights lifted from its perch. Then he rubbed the clear skin of his forehead and kept rubbing until finally, he burst into tears. "No! It shouldn't have been me. I didn't need it. I didn't find it. I don't deserve it, either. I'm a criminal."

"You're a boy," the dancer said with a shake of his head. "The rest of us have done something with our lives, and you should have the chance to do the same. One mistake shouldn't take that away from you forever."

"It wasn't one mistake. I often poach from the King's forests."

For some reason, that set the adults all chuckling, many of them glancing at the old man. "Well, I happen to know the King," the dancer said at last, "and I'm sure he could find a place for you among his own hunters. Didn't you say you were the best?"

"Sure I am, but isn't the King mad?"

"Of course not."

The artist and the dancer got to their feet together, arms wrapped around each other's waists, and the dancer contradicted her by saying, "He is a little bit." As he spoke, the old man and the boy stood up beside them, and the daughter joined the knot of them and grasped the worn handles of her mother's chair.

"He's so mad," the dancer continued, "that he thought one boy would be able to find his way to us through a magic fairy maze."

"I wasn't that far away, and besides, I'm the best ..." He stopped as understanding dawned. "Oh." He didn't know what else to say to that, or to say to the King who called him here.

Explanations would wait. He had a place if he wanted it, just like they all did. They all had plans for the future and, even more importantly, hope. It often happened that way. This time, all it took for me to nudge them together was a flower, some fairy breath, and a little rerouting. The rest was up to them, as it always was.

The boy began to replace the cap on his head out of habit but then stopped himself and shoved it back in his pocket. "What do we do now?" he asked his King.

The old man swept his hand toward the hedges that surrounded the garden and replied, "Exit the fairy maze."

The Fairy
and the
Flower

KRISTIN TOWE

Spring had just whispered its way into the little meadow where the fairies live, as it always does, quietly and sweetly, with none of the aggressiveness of winter, and all the fair folk were beginning their yearly migration from the stouter tree hollows into their more delicate homes—the flowers.

"Mariposa," a fairy named Florinia twittered from the inside of a spacious tulip, "Do you need any help with those?"

Mariposa, with wings fluttering like Victorian eyelashes, was having a difficult time staying in the air with her arms so full of her belongings. One very heavy thimble persistently bumped up against her flute, and she kept having to swoop down and catch a moccasin or two before they fell into the dirt.

"No, I'm—" the thimble, in a final act of rebellion, teetered and then fell directly on top of her head.

Florinia, faithful friend that she was, swooped down and helped Mariposa out of the dirt, lifting the thimble off her head and dusting off her wings.

"Moving day is always so stressful," Mariposa moaned, flying slightly higher now that Florinia had helped carry some of her things.

"Why do you keep carrying this with you, anyway?" Florinia questioned, nodding her head in the direction of the thimble. "It has never worked before, and it's always such a nuisance. Besides, the flowers despise that metal taste."

It was a question that all the fairies of the meadow continued to ask, and rightfully so. You see, faeries in this part of the world were born from a baby's first laugh, and, in rare cases, the faeries would take on gifts of the babies they were born from. This was becoming more and more uncommon, however, and Mariposa was the only fairy in her meadow who had been affected this way.

The baby whose laughter she had been born from had the gift of music in its blood, and this gift had been shared with her. When Mariposa sang or played any sort of instrument, she could invoke whatever emotion she pleased upon a person. Unfortunately, the baby also carried the curse of the artist—a tendency toward violent mood swings which manifested within Mariposa as nightmares.

Since her entry into life, she had been trying desperately to rid herself of this curse, testing everything from psychoanalytic treatments, to herbal concoctions, and finally, to consulting with a witch. The witch advised her to empty her thoughts into the thimble each night and postulated that, with time, her nightmares would turn into sweet dreams. Mariposa had been doing this for two years now, however, and no change had yet occurred.

Everyone in the meadow, the flowers especially, wanted her to abandon the thimble, but it was the only hope she had, and she clung to it stubbornly.

"Well, damn the flowers!" Mariposa huffed, ears turning bright red as the two began to flutter down to the grass in front of her new spring home. "I wake up as yellow as a warbler every morning because of their filthy pollen, and it takes me ages to wash it all off."

Wide-eyed, Florinia looked up at the rose-bush that Mariposa would be living in for the rest of Spring.

"Shh!" she whispered in fright. "You really need to quit cursing the flowers. They will mutiny against us all, and then we'll have to resort back to living under toadstools!"

With that, Florinia gave her friend a peck on the cheek and fluttered away, leaving Mariposa standing at the base of a bush of crimson roses. The sweet, organic smell caressed her nose, and she closed her eyes, allowing herself to flutter towards the rose that smelled sweetest to her. Each one smelled nice, like bottled wishes and pomegranates, but one smelled different, like the familiar scent of a lover's hair, like salty kisses shared under rumpled sheets. She followed the smell until she reached its source and opened her eyes. To her untrained eye, it did not appear to be any different than the rest, but its perfume was intoxicating, and without a bit of restraint, she tumbled down into her new home. Her head rested against the rose's voluptuous silk petals, and she let out a tiny sigh of pleasure.

"Home," she whispered into the flower's satin center.

Nobody is completely certain, but the legend goes that the rose gave a tiny sigh as well.

🌿 🌿

Mariposa awoke with a start and blinked her eyes against the mid-afternoon sun.

"Shit!" she shouted, causing some startled eyes to peek out at her from their nearby flowers.

She had not intended to take a nap, in fact, because of the nightmares, she avoided sleep as much as she could, and instead, she threw herself into her work. She was a musician, and in a world of faeries, her music-making talent was always in high demand. In fact, from the way the sun was positioned in the sky, it appeared that she was late for the Parade of the Great Move, a spring tradition in which she was always featured, and one that she would be missing if she did not hurry to get there. In a dash,

Mariposa fluttered down to the ground, grabbed her suitcase, and opened it. She pulled out a bright red, sequined dress, and closing the petals of the rose around her, stripped off her clothes. She quickly changed, flew back down to the ground where she had left the rest of her belongings, grabbed her flute, and fluttered wildly toward the location of the parade. It was not until after a few minutes of flying had passed that she realized, for the first time in years, she had slept without a single nightmare.

※ ※

"Huzzah! She's here!" a group of male fairies, ridiculously sotted, called out as Mariposa fluttered frantically over them to the area where the musicians gathered for their performances. There was only one person left to perform, and being the closing musician, she had made it just in time.

"So you decided to show up after all," murmured a sultry voice from between smug lips. It was Fenwick, next in line and a skilled fiddler who also happened to be the main person Mariposa would turn to in her drunken hours for a midnight fairy-frolic. She found him attractive, but only in a superficial way.

"Hello, Fenwick," Mariposa muttered in an annoyed voice, all the while letting her gaze linger on the way his dress shirt clung to the muscles in his arms.

The upbeat drum medley of the fairy who was currently playing came to an abrupt end, and the already drunken crowd began to bellow their requests for more music. Fenwick reached for his fiddle and then leaned toward Mariposa.

"Find me later," he whispered in her ear, giving it a tiny nibble before he pulled himself away.

Mariposa rolled her eyes, trying to seem disinterested, but the raspberry hue that had appeared on her face gave her away.

With a wink, Fenwick sauntered away from her and onto the stage, and the joyful music of his rapid fingers against the fiddle saturated the meadow air.

While Mariposa was standing there, contemplating what she should play on her flute and also admiring how Fenwick managed to squeeze his legs into such small trousers, a soft buzzing sound began to interrupt her thoughts, followed by a voice she had never heard before, *Think of me.*

Startled, Mariposa looked around to see what witch or magician had been allowed to the festivities and was playing a trick on her, but there was none in sight. The voice disappeared, and so did the cheerful refrain of the fiddle medley. So, absolutely befuddled, Mariposa forced her confusion aside and fluttered onto the stage, flute poised at her lips.

If you have never attended a fairy parade before, here is what you should know, golden fairy dust drips from the collective flutter of hundreds of wings like a magic snowfall, lighting the air so that no other form of light is necessary. There is music so wild and natural that it tastes like honey on your tongue, and there are tables of food, spread out underneath the moonlight, laden with blue-berries, honeycombs, hazelnuts, and everything else that faeries find exceptionally delicious. There is also nectar, the alcoholic beverage of choice among faeries, served from human-sized kettles, and by seven o'clock, every fairy in attendance is drunk.

By the time Mariposa took the stage, the nectar kettles had been almost emptied. Faeries naturally have excessive amounts of energy, but all of that becomes more accelerated under the influence of alcohol, and the crowd in front of her was beginning to grow rowdy.

She had begun to play a fairy jig, but the mood of the crowd was becoming too violent and bawdy for dancing. When she saw some drunken idiot try to put his hands on Florinia, something snapped inside of her, and she knew what she had to do. She took a deep breath, whispered to herself the word 'peace,' and began to play a soft, tinkling combination from her flute.

The air around her began to tingle, and she knew that her magic was working. She continued. Quiet began to fall over the crowd around her, and she could see both Florinia and the drunken idiot standing with serene smiles on their faces. The catcalling had stopped, the shoving had ceased, and peace reigned once more over the festivities. When her song came to an end, Mariposa gave a curtsey in response to the crowd's applause and then fluttered away, exhausted from the magic that had just been drained out of her.

Her wings were drooping, and she decided to just return home when out of the corner of her eye, she saw Fenwick approaching.

"Turn around, Fenwick. I am not in the mood."

"Look what I have, though." He grinned up at her boorishly. In his hands was a wooden cup filled with a delicious smelling beverage. "It's the last cup of nectar."

Although it was tempting, Mariposa turned it down, wanting nothing more than the comfort of her silky flower bed.

"Come on, Mari. Have some fun." The look she gave him in response shut him up for a few seconds, and he flew silently beside her until she reached the threshold of her rosebush. "Well, if you are really tired, I could join you."

The rakish grin he gave her—and the sight of his muscular calves bulging out of his pants legs—was, like the nectar, extremely tempting, but instead, she gave him a playful shove and told him to go home.

Yet, when she flew up to her rose, he was still following her. She could smell the stale nectar on his breath and see an angry, determined glint in his amber eyes. Fear began to settle in the pit of her stomach, but it manifested itself as anger.

"I am serious, Fenwick! Go away. You are drunk, and I don't want anything to do with you."

Fenwick reached to grab her when, all of a sudden, the rosebush began to shake. A thorn-studded stem coiled itself around Fenwick's leg, and he yelped in pain, giving

Mariposa the opportunity to jump into the rose for safety. It curled its soft petals around her, and once again, she sighed, knowing she was completely safe.

"Thank you," she whispered, nuzzling her head against the silken petals, breathing in their lovely, comforting scent.

She heard Fenwick struggle to disentangle his leg and then fly away, muttering a few expletives and the name of some other girl who would be more than willing to share a drunken flower-frolic with him, and she shook her head in disgust. Sleep began to collect in her eyes, and her breathing settled. Right before she fell asleep, she heard the same buzzing sound from earlier followed by a voice that sounded as familiar as home.

Goodnight, Mariposa. Sweet dreams.

❧ ❧

And sweet dreams, she had. In fact, after she had wiped the sleep out of her eyes, she realized that she had left her thimble for collecting nightmares on the ground with the rest of her things for the entirety of the night. It was the first time in two years she hadn't used it, and it was the first time in all of her life that she had slept through the night without a single bad dream.

Strange energy seemed to emanate from the rose once she began to move around. It felt to her like the flower was excited that she was awake, like her existence brought it joy. She dressed and decided that it was time to bring in the rest of her belongings, which currently lay sprawled beneath her in the dirt. Mariposa fluttered back and forth, dropping off shoes, clothes, and random other necessities until all that was left on the ground was the thimble.

"Do I need it anymore?" She bemused. A part of her wanted to take it, just as security, but she knew how the flowers reacted to metal, and though it had never bothered her in the past, for some reason she was loathed to irritate this particular rose. Unsure, she fluttered back up to her flower, reclined against its velvet backing, and turned to her flute to help her sort out the confusion of everything that was going on around her. It was still early morning, and everyone around her had stayed late at the parade and were sleeping soundly, so she played soft lullabies, all the while wondering about the voice she had been hearing lately and the sudden disappearance of her nightmares, wondering if there was a correlation between the two.

You are upset.

Mariposa, no longer startled by the appearance of the voice, wanted desperately to communicate with it, so, as silly as it made her feel, she whispered out into the dark nothingness of early morning.

"Who are you?" Her voice was like a tinkling bell, timid birdsong, and the excitement that had been radiating from the rose pulsed at the sound of it.

Let me show you.

The heady, freshly-unbottled wine fragrance of the rose that she had begun to grow accustomed to grew stronger, and as she breathed it in, a warmth filled her body, easing her confusion. Her eyes grew heavy, and the flute fell into her lap as her hands and body slacked in complete relaxation. In the way that honey melts smoothly off a hot spoon, the vision that was being given to her melted into the darkness of her closed eyes, staining them with color.

She appeared to be nestled somewhere between stems and leaves, somehow weightless and yet rooted to a force as old as time itself. Every sound was amplified; a ladybug landed on a leaf across the meadow, and she could hear its legs tickle the grass as it moved. She also heard two voices, but the other didn't matter at all—it was as inconsequential as the morning dew. It was the second that caused a strange thrill, like the movement of ash on the ground before the phoenix emerges, reborn. "Well, damn the flowers!" The voice cried. She suddenly felt a sense of urgency, a need to be near the voice, to know its owner. Knowing the ritual of the faeries on moving day, all that could be done was to let his petals become unfurled, releasing his perfume, and hope that she chose him. So when she did, when her body relaxed against his open arms, and she sighed against him, he reveled in the joy of being chosen—of knowing that the connection he felt for her had been returned. He vowed to care and protect her in whatever way he could.

The vision blurred for a second, then changed into mid-afternoon.

He had been watching her, following her through the roots that spread throughout all the earth, already unwilling to be separated from her. She was standing under the solid oak, behind a stage, and there was a male fairy beside her. He felt carnal longing radiate from her, but no love. Still, it pained his heart to see her desire someone—like a prick of a thorn against delicate skin. Out of this pain, he sent his voice up to her. *Think of me.* He saw her bewildered response and hated to frighten her, but the connection he felt for her was stronger even than the roots that held him captive to the earth, and he didn't want her to waste her heart on lust when he knew he could offer her a love more solid than the ground itself. As he watched her play her flute, he thought of her that afternoon, the first time she had slept within his arms, and of how he had fought back the dark magic that tried to leak in through his petals to attack her dreams. He would go on protecting her from the nightmares for as long as she would let him.

Once again, the vision blurred, and then it was nighttime.

The cricket song quickly faded into oblivion, like all else did, at the sound of her voice. "I am serious, Fenwick! Go away! You are drunk, and I don't want anything to do with you." *I will kill him*, he hissed as everything began to turn red. Rage-filled, he flicked a thorn branch around the villainous male fairy's leg and opened his arms wide for Mariposa to fall into. Once she was safe, he closed his petals tightly around her and released a perfume that would bring her peace and comfort. Ambivalent to the male fairy, who was struggling to free himself, all his attention turned toward her. She smelled of fine-art, of a masterpiece that belonged in a gilded frame, and when she burrowed her head up into his chest, his heart ached out of an abundance of love.

Love, love, love ... The word clung to her ears as the effect of the vision began to fade away, and she opened her eyes back up to the darkness of the morning. More scared and confused than she was before, Mariposa pushed open the rose's petals and flitted away as quickly as her wings would carry her.

❧ ❧

"Florinia! Get up! I need you!" Mariposa whispered frantically into the petals of her friend's home. The petals suddenly opened, and she couldn't help but wonder if her rose had sent a message through the earth to this flower, once again acting on her behalf no matter the distance. Mariposa stuck her arm into the plump little tulip and extracted Florinia from her bed.

There is a place in the fairy meadow where nature makes gentle music all the day long—the river—and this is where Mariposa dragged her half-asleep friend. She was hoping the sound of the rambling water might prevent the rose from hearing what she said.

Florinia, who had just fluttered down to sit on a rock by the water, stretched her arms and released a yawn.

"Alright, then, Mari. What is this all about?"

She sat quietly as Mariposa explained everything, spewing her words out as rapidly as teakettle steam. When she explained the voice she had been hearing, Florinia jumped a little, and whenever she mentioned the rose giving her visions, she fell off the rock into a puddle and had to flutter her wings to dry them off, but still, she remained silent.

"... and I can't deny that I do feel some unexplainable connection to him, but he is a flower! A flower! I mean, really, how would a relationship like that ever work?"

"I don't know much about love," Florinia murmured with sympathy spilling from her eyes, "but I know that instant, unexplainable connections rarely come in life. But besides that, Mariposa, love is love. Does it really matter in what form it comes to you?"

Mariposa looked at her friend, and her eyes, which up to the moment had been wild with uncertainty, suddenly calmed, along with her breathing.

"He brings you peace, and he protects you. Your nightmares have finally gone away. You get what I'm saying, right?"

She got it—completely—which is why at that moment she kissed her friend farewell and shot off with as much speed as a cannon, flying urgently toward her flower, her home. Upon arrival, she noticed something was off. The scent of the rose that she had become so familiar with was barely noticeable, and as she approached him, she could see his petals were drooped.

I didn't think you would return to me.

She settled herself back into the rose and leaned into his velvet embrace.

"And, yet, here I am," she whispered, words timidly tiptoeing off her tongue.

Why? The uncertainty in his voice pained her and spurred her to action.

"Let me show you."

Mariposa reached for her flute and put it to her lips. A song of love and gratitude and decision began to dance through the air, soft as butterfly wings at first, but eventually growing into all the heated passion of a forest fire, a passion that had been felt for her, a passion that she now returned.

While she was playing, something strange began to happen with the rose. His petals, which had begun to sag at the thought of losing her, perked up, and up, and up until they rose completely in the air and Mariposa was left sitting on the stem.

Frightened, she wanted to quit playing, but the flute stuck to her lips and a force greater than herself compelled her onwards. The petals pirouetted in the air and then converged into a glowing orb of light. At the very climax of her song, the orb exploded, and golden fairy dust rained from the sky all around her.

The flute fell from her shaking hands, hands that she brought to cover her mouth, to stifle the sobs that threatened to bring her to despair. At that moment, she thought her song of love had killed her gentle rose.

But then she saw him—golden hair waved back from a somehow familiar face, and new wings, glowing in the pale light of the rising sun, fluttering straight toward her. A tiny pinprick of uncertainty plagued her as she looked at him. Was this really her rose, somehow transformed into a fairy? That uncertainty faded away as he got nearer to her, as his heady and familiar scent danced in the air around her. He flew toward her, closer, until he was only an inch away from her face, and rested his hands on her neck.

"Mariposa." His voice was as velvet-soft as his petal embrace once was.

"How ... what ... did I—" she stuttered, slightly delirious with confusion and happiness.

"Dearest, never doubt the transformative power of true love."

With that, he kissed her, and the nectar of his lips tasted like the dispelling of nightmares, like the sweetest of dreams.

True love can come in many forms.

Natural Enemies

AKASYA BENGE

The fox King decided this would be the day to end the war with the wolves.

This war began before the time of the oldest fox's grandfather. It began when the paths of the fox and the wolf diverged along the road of evolution, and the two nations decided one would be the hunter and the other the trickster. They were natural enemies.

"Send a delegation to trap a wolf," ordered the King. This may not seem like the normal job of a delegation, but the King knew any fox sent into the den of the wolves would not come out alive, and the foxes were clever enough to avoid this. It was better to capture one and make him take the message.

Six foxes were chosen, each for different attributes. One was swift, another cunning, one large and strong. Another was flexible, one more was knowledgeable, and the last was the most important. The tiny white Princess, despite her elegance and size, had all the talents foxes held in great esteem.

Deep in the forest, they gathered.

"We must," said the Princess, "appeal to what wolves need most."

"That is easy," growled the large, husky grey fox. He had lost an eye years ago, and his remaining one burned with all the intensity that two should have. "We must set a trap with bleeding, fresh, meat."

"No," said the Princess. "They can survive weeks without meat. What we must do is cut off their water supply."

Most people do not know that a wolf must drink water each and every day to survive. They think as long as they have something to feast upon they need nothing else. Most foxes think this as well, yet the Princess knew better. She knew that wolves are beasts of feast and famine.

So the foxes hurriedly began to search the forest for the source of the wolves' water. In order to hide their identity, each fox wore a mask and darted purposefully among the trees.

The woods were full of hidden pools whose water came from mysterious sources. However, all were in the territory of the foxes. Only one river ran continually through the forest, the living barrier between the two nations. As this river also ran through their den, the wolves hardly bothered to worry about the pools of the foxes.

The Princess knew she would have to find a far away source to blockade the stream. Build anything too close to the wolves, and they risked being eaten or having the wolves simply break apart their work. She also knew a trap must be ready at the pond closest to the border.

The foxes piled rocks into that pond and began to dig a hole close by. They dug it deep and wide enough to capture a wolf, and to keep him alive until they could convince him to be their new envoy. They only wanted one wolf, for who knew what the power of two could do. Over this hole, the Princess lay very thin slices of a transparent material she knew broke easily. It is known as the mineral mica to humans, and the fox Princess was very clever indeed in how she collected the thinnest layers and wove them together, so when the wolf came to drink at this 'pond,' he would fall right through. This trap would have fooled no fox, but the delegation knew it would work with a wolf.

When their beautiful trap was completed, the scouts reported back to the Princess that they found a suitable spot to temporarily stop the water flow. They found a small but powerful waterfall several miles from the den of the wolves. Quickly the six foxes converged on the spot, and within a few hours, were able to stop the flow of the river with giant rocks they rolled in.

Then they hid in the trees near their trap and waited.

And waited.

And waited.

Eventually, a wolf of unusual color and sleekness stepped cautiously from the woods. For it was one thing for a wolf to seek his prey in this land, and quite another for him to seek water and survival, so he slunk from the forest with dread outlined in each paw print made on the freshly upturned earth. He did not notice the sunken ground, he only crept closer to the shining, shimmering space that promised water and relief from his parched throat.

He fell into the trap.

As he howled, all six converged around the hole to peer in.

The wolf snarled and snapped in the depths of the dark hole, too angry to speak. Five of the six went away to remove the rocks from the waterfall and start the river again before more wolves came. The Princess lay next to the hole and listened to the sounds of the trapped wolf.

"LET ME OUT!" he roared.

"No," said the fox Princess.

"LET ME OUT, OR I WILL EAT YOU!" he roared.

"If I let you out you will eat me," the Princess replied.

He growled his acknowledgment and desire to do so.

"I will bring you food and water," said the Princess, "so that you may find some relief."

The Princess brought the supplies she had hidden and pushed them into the hole. For a while, only the sounds of slurping and gnawing could be heard.

When there was silence again, the Princess asked, "Are you hurt?"

The wolf shifted and rattled within his fox-made cage, "No."

The sounds of the river began again, and the five other foxes returned.

"What will we do now Princess?" asked a slender red fox. He could get in and out of almost any space, and he had discovered the optimum point to block the waterfall.

"We will report to the King of our success, and slowly, we will get this wolf to understand the ways of the fox, so that he can plead our case well with the Wolf Queen."

The wolf below overheard and barked noises like ill-tempered laughter. "The Wolf Queen will not hear my plea. I am the lowest of the wolves, because of my small size and my strange fur. No one will listen to me."

The Princess looked down at the wretched creature she had captured. "I will teach you to be clever as a fox, and if nothing else, your people will not eat you, for you are a wolf. If they are wise, they will want to hear from a wolf who has lived among foxes."

Again the wolf laughed, "What wolf is wise?" he asked.

※ ※

The King was very pleased with their progress and allowed the Princess to continue with her plan. The next day the Princess returned to the hole, to find the wolf sleeping. She once again lay down beside the hole and waited for him to awake. When he did, he seemed calmer than the day before. "Here is food and water again," said the Princess. She lowered it down with a vine and her teeth. The wolf ate without comment.

"Do you want to hear a story?" she asked. The wolf made no reply. She continued, "It is one we tell all fox children."

Still, the wolf said nothing.

"Then I will tell you of Reynard the Fox and Bruin the Bear, and how Reynard stole honey from right under the nose of his friend the bear ..."

Each day the Princess returned and told the wolf stories told to all fox children to help them learn to think in clever ways. She fed him and gave him water, and wondered why no wolf came searching for him.

"What is your name?" she asked the wolf.

"The other wolves gave me no name," he replied.

"Would you like one?" she asked. He just looked at her with eyes that still glowed yellow amongst his slowly darkening, matted fur. "I will give you the name of a hero then ... Reynard."

Then she called the other five foxes to her. "Help me get him out!" she commanded. She was brave enough to make this command because she knew he would be too weak to run. They lifted him out, and indeed, the wolf could not move much. He stank of the hole, and so the Princess ordered to take him to a shallow portion of the river. There they washed him with honey and fed him some more, and then took him to a sunny glade in the forest where he could be warm and dry.

The wolf struggled to stand, but he seemed to welcome the tender care the foxes gave him. He sat silently again, the Princess near him so he would not run. She commanded they tie his neck with the strongest vine, and wrap it one hundred times around a tree. Now the wolf could not run, but he could walk. The Princess organized the five other foxes so that there would always be a guard. She then rose, and said to the wolf, "Goodnight, Reynard."

He looked at her, his beautiful and unusual fur now clean and fresh, and smelling of flowers. Despite the fact his legs were weak, his fur and body seemed fuller now than when he had first come to the mica pool. "Goodnight, Princess," he replied.

The next day she returned and said, "Today I will tell you the story of Reynard the Fox and Isengrim the Wolf."

So she told the story of the dastardly Isengrim and the clever Reynard. She told the most elaborate, cleverest versions of the stories she knew and had heard so many times as a cub herself. Finally, when they were over, with the wolf's steady gaze on her, she waited for him to say something.

"You are beautiful," said the wolf.

Now it was the Princess's turn to be silent.

The two did not notice the red fox watching them from his narrow perch in a tree.

From that day the Princess felt a change in her heart, and she returned to the wolf more full of feeling than purpose. With the steady supply of food and grooming the foxes provided, his fur grew more luxurious and softer, and his eyes lost their manic and desperate edge. He began to even look like a fox, for his face grew more clever with the Princess's stories and other lessons she gave him, as she was full of knowledge and wonder for the world around her. One day she ventured to creep towards him and give him an encouraging lick for remembering what she had said the day before.

Swiftly he lay his foreleg across her side, trapping her beneath his powerful body. She thought she would die in that instant, but instead, she felt the warm roughness of his tongue against her fur. She relaxed and nuzzled against his now wonderful coat. They fell asleep in the glade that day, side by side, without fear. The Princess returned home with a feeling like fire in her chest that night and tossed and turned thinking of the wolf in the moonlight.

She returned to the glade the next day with a plan.

"If the two nations of fox and wolf are to no longer be enemies, there must be important and solidifying alliances made between them," she said to him.

The wolf, who had just eaten his breakfast of fresh fish, said, "I agree."

The Princess felt nervous. She continued on saying, "If you can convince the Wolf Queen to end the war, I know my father will allow you to return here in a position of honor … and you may stay with me."

The wolf seemed pleased. "I agree to this, too."

"Good," replied the Princess. "Now we must continue with your lessons so we may succeed and end this war."

So for many, many days, the wolf remained with the foxes. Eventually, they released him from his glade, and it became common to see the wolf side by side with the Princess among the foxes. The King, who had seemed in no rush early on, did gently remind his daughter that perhaps now the wolf was ready to carry out his mission. But the Princess now deeply feared what might happen. She knew there was no reason to worry, for a wolf will not hurt one of its own pack. They would surely welcome the wolf they must have thought dead. She insisted again and again that he was not ready, that he had not learned all the ways of the foxes.

It took the death of one of the foxes for the King to finally order the wolf away. He was one of the King's best knights and the flexible red fox of the team of six. He had been the favorite of the people for the Princess's hand, and now they began to fear for the future of their nation. He had gone into the wolf's land to find out more about Reynard, for he had been jealous of the attention the Princess had been giving him. Many foxes came and pleaded with the King for action, and despite knowing of the ambiguous fears that lay in the Princess' heart, he summoned her to lead the wolf to the edge of their lands at sunrise.

The Princess returned to the wolf's grove, where he now lay meekly in the sun, watching butterflies as they landed on the edge of his nose, and nestled between feather tufts of rusty colored fur. The Princess's heart ached as she lay against her handsome companion, wishing he would never, ever leave her. He soothed her. "I will be back soon," he said. "Then I will never leave you, and the King will never want me to leave you again."

The Princess said nothing and wished that he would be right.

The next morning, the wolf, freshly washed with honey and water and with a belly full of fish, walked into the wolf nation, and then along the river, to the den of the wolves. There he remembered all the old smells and habits of his life there and asked for an audience with the Queen. The wolves descended.

"What is this?" one asked, saliva falling between razor-edged exposed teeth.

"This is not a wolf," said another.

The wolf began to be afraid.

"He smells of honey," said another. "What wolf smells of honey and walks with grace?"

"You know what I am," said the wolf, "though you gave me no name and only the most rancid of scraps and dirtiest of bones to live on. I too may ask for an audience with the Queen."

The noise of the snapping, snarling wolves drew the attention of their Queen, and she stepped out, expansive and dark as a midwinter night. From her stone ledge above, she looked down at the creature who was clean and well-fed, without disease or desperation.

"I know you," said the Queen. "You were our fool."

"My lady—" began the wolf.

"More the fool now," said the Queen. "Do with him as you would any of his kind."

The wolves circled around Reynard, trapping him in.

For the foxes had been too clever for the wolves.

The transformation was so complete, Reynard looked like a fox, he smelled like fox ... and, in the end, he tasted like a fox too.

Journey to the Abyss

JACK E. MOHR

NOW

I stand at the abyss—the air stiff and rigid. I am unencumbered, undaunted, and unenlightened. I don't know what to expect, but my expectations are high. Any knowledge I've acquired about the Abyss has been from rumor and conjecture. No one who has entered has lived to speak about it.

Yet, I am ready, perfectly ready to enter my destiny.

I look down at the Abyss, and it looks back at me apathetically.

A thin proportioned boy, near the age of eleven, stood at the edge of an arid landmass—clothing tattered. Heat emanated from the molting darkness while he stood undaunted and undeterred. No one was in sight. Not a sign of life. The atmosphere felt motionless, and all that remained was him and his brooding destiny. His breaths were deep, and his heartbeat slowed. The darkness hypnotized him into a trancelike lull. Tears budded.

He peered into what could be, and he thought back on what was. His life had been the culmination of tribulations and grueling testaments—one after another—like a Greek folktale. He suffered scars, none of which remain. All that remained was a boy, a beetle, and a purpose—his purpose, pure and exact.

His body was adorned with trophies that represented the success of his trials and ordeals. He wore the skull of a Myer Ram on the crown of his head. No ordinary Myer Ram—a King's skull. It possessed a particular power—a magic that the boy harnessed but didn't fully understand. Through his veins coursed the blood of a Sebastian Serpent along with the venom of a Tarchnede Arachnid, both of which provided a unique power.

He had experienced so much. There was a time when he would have considered those experiences to only be the myths of fantasy and folklore. That was until he witnessed those events and had shed blood for things men considered to be of fairy tales. All those events molded him for this moment, and he could now fulfill the perfection that fate provided.

FOUR BLOOD MOONS PRIOR

"How did you get here child?" a very groggy voice whispered.

The boy could not move or speak, he could only panic. A flush of heat rushed across his face as his imagination attempted to match a face with the voice. He strained to move his head and created enough wiggle to view the creature. His eyes bulged when he saw a gaunt, tall, and thinly built humanoid. The bones of its arms and legs were exposed and ivory colored. Antiquated, they cracked with each movement. A light green moss resembling sheep's wool covered the being's torso.

The creature was a female Myer Ram but unrecognizeably so. She wasn't burly, fleshed out in muscle with a thick hide. On the contrary, her body was devoid of muscle, and her bones almost appeared wooden, as though she had absorbed the traits of the forest. Her appearance was odd, but the fact that she was alone was even odder. Myer Rams were always seen with the herd and were not known to survive without it.

The boy had been ensnared within the web of a grand Tarchnede Arachnid for quite some time before the Myer Ram arrived. The web was constructed of a sticky adhesive substance, and its massive strands could make a bear appear the size of a fly. Not even a finger could be lifted. He couldn't decide who to fear more—the creature or the arachnid—he just hoped his fate would be painless.

The Myer Ram looked down on the child and took a liking. He was out of place, like a sheep among a pack of wolves, but she possessed an innate desire for things that were out of place. There was a time when she felt out of place—until she vowed to make a place of her own out of any place she desired to be. Her compassion for the child guided her actions.

She resided within the Forbidden Forest and wandered freely without fear, confining to the laws of magic being her only constraint. No one was exempt from the ills the forest had to offer because death roamed freest of all. And right now, one of those ills presented imminent danger.

Happenstance delayed the boy from being devoured—luckily for him, the Tarchnede Arachnid was busy watching her eggs hatch. Fortunately for him, a certain Myer Ram saw something worth saving. The horns of a Myer Ram possessed a power—a power none understood but most respected.

"How did you get here child?" the ram repeated.

She attempted to tap into the boy's mind, but his panic made it impossible. He was unresponsive like a startled deer. She tenderly removed sweat from the boy's brow. Her warmth put him at ease, while her fragrance settled his thoughts—a distinct rosemary savor.

The boy's panic gradually subsided, and she attuned her mind's eye with his mental images. His thoughts consisted of his toilsome journey, and were dark, without joy. She no longer wanted to view these images and acted quickly. Carefully, she levitated, hoping to conceal her presence from the spider. With precision, she used her horns to slice the boy free.

The web's vibration alerted the arachnid. Most of her eggs had hatched, and her hatchlings followed as she sought to discern the intrusion. With dozens of baby spiders entangled in her black hair, she livened her pace towards the boy. The sight of the Myer Ram immediately halted her charge and her four largest red eyes locked onto the unrelenting stare of the Myer Ram, and their mind's exchanged thoughts.

"How dare you defy the laws that death has placed before us!" expressed the arachnid.

"This boy is an anomaly, and laws do not apply to the abnormal!" expressed the ram.

The arachnid responded with a loud shriek, knocking the Myer Ram out of the air. The ram regained her composure and charged towards the boy, as did the arachnid. With all of her might, the Myer Ram lunged towards the child. The arachnid lunged and sank a venomous fang into his leg. As the Myer Ram pulled him free, the fang dug deeper. The Myer Ram released a piercing sound from her horns that dislodged the fang.

Unfortunately, the poison's effects were swift and unforgiving. A pungent smell of rotting flesh festered. The child winced.

"Shhh, Shhh," she rocked him in her arms as she whisked him away. She attuned herself with the boy which allowed her to absorb his pain. Unfortunately it did not stop the venom's effects. The arachnid did not pursue. She was powerless outside of her web and would become as mortal as the next without its aura.

"It will be okay. The venom can take your body, it can take your mind, but as long as it does not reach your soul, all the damage that is done can be undone," expressed the Myer Ram.

"What? How are we communicating? What's going on?" he thought.

The child felt his soul detaching from his mind and body. The strands of essence that were keeping him together were slowly pulling apart. He lost control of his bodily functions as his mind's perception became warped. He no longer smelled the reassurance of rosemary. He no longer felt the warmth of the ram's embrace. He couldn't even smell the rotting of his flesh or taste the bitter residue of salt from his sweat. It was as though he was in a bubble separated from his senses.

"My name is Selma; we must heal you quickly."

With enough space between her and the web, Selma descended to the forest floor and planted her hooves firmly on the ground. She stomped rhythmically, creating a vibrational pattern. As she did so, the amulet around her neck gently brushed back and forth against the boy. She evoked a melodic whistling with her horns and the two frequencies merged as one creating a portal. Embracing the boy securely, Selma levitated, glided through the portal, and it quickly dissolved behind her.

The portal transported the pair to a unique part of the forest. It possessed very little light, which emanated from the bioluminescence of the surrounding foliage. She gently placed the boy on his back atop a grass clearing.

"What is your name, child?"

Selma continued communicating through his thoughts. Despite no longer possessing the physical function to respond, he retained the ability to evoke thought. His thoughts created images that Selma viewed with her mind's eye.

"Aww ... Antiochticus, what a proud and unique name. Antiochticus, we will have you healed in no time."

Selma rested on bended knee perpendicular to the boy. She leaned down and kissed his forehead. In very melodic-guttural tones she chanted.

"Asha ... Ashe ... ashaaa-asheee ... ASHaaa—ASHeee ..."

A magic was evoked that most would never understand. Ant-sized fairies sprouted from the grass. Selma's eye was lured by the glow of their wings. One by one the fairies appeared. By nature, they were very playful and loved to play tricks—they took very little serious. Yet, they immediately sensed the urgency of the situation. Pink, the leader of the Ganza fairies, came forward as a representative to speak.

"Selma ... Long time no di si. Pleasure! Ooo looky dere, you bringey boy. Di boy do not look very good, he needy di help!"

"Delighted to see you as well, Pink. It's true, I'm afraid the boy isn't doing well. In fact, it's the very reason you were summoned." replied Selma

"Sure you right Di. Hmm ... What Di got for me?" asked Pink.

Along with being tricksters, the fairies were master negotiators and never let an opportunity to haggle pass. They easily read the situation and recognized an opportunity.

Selma recalled the first time she met Pink. It was shortly after she arrived in the forest, the fairies had seen that she was hungry, desperate, alone, and they used that as the perfect chance to capture Selma within their debts. From that point on, Selma knew she could trust the fairies, but it would always come at an unbalanced price.

"This is rather an unexpected and desperate situation. Surely you do have pity?" asked Selma.

"Di di di di di, we me's do's have hearts ..." said Pink as he scratched his chin.

"Well, all I have to offer is what you see."

"Di Di Di ... Di Di ... I spy something shiny. Di Der neck posses a power Di want."

Selma clutched the amulet around her neck. "What could you possibly want with this old thing? You aren't even big enough to wear it."

"Don't worry Di Der bery little hooves," Pink said with a smile. All the fairies' wings flickered in excitement.

Selma placed great sentiment with the amulet and did not want to part with it. This wasn't the fairies first attempt at her amulet. She went through tremendous efforts to obtain the amulet and rather often utilized the power it possessed. She knew the Ganza fairies recognized its power, and she understood she was being taken advantage of. But she was stuck and couldn't escape the dilemma. Something innate persuaded Selma to believe the boy was vital. Vital to what? She wasn't sure. But she maintained faith in her intuition, it had yet to fail her.

"Fine."

"Di Di Di Di Di!!" Pink shouted, and all the Ganza joined in jubilant unison. Selma removed the amulet from around her neck and laid it on top of several Ganza. Like little ants, they carried the amulet away and they, along with the amulet, absorbed back into the earth.

"Now, your end of the bargain?"

"Di end? You no ask no Ding of us. Di Di Di."

Selma wanted so bad to be filled with anger, despite knowing the trickster nature of the Ganza. She didn't have it in her to even feign anger. Before she responded, she heard a buzzing noise. The unseen honey bees of Galoria, in a single-file line, appeared from nowhere. They flew by Selma's head and landed on top of Antiochticus. Seven of the worker bees created a circle on the boy's forehead—the same spot that Semla had kissed.

"Thank you, Pink." Selma's tone was contrite.

"A life for a life ... Di Di Di Di." Pink submerged into the forest floor. The honey bees created a melody with the flapping of their wings. The melody painted an expression in the air—rich, verbose and full of illuminating-vibrant color. Within the melody, Selma saw the bee's story and understood their sacrifice. In unison, the flapping stopped and the atmosphere darkened.

One by one the thirteen bees stung the child's forehead, their stingers detached from their bodies as did their lives. The stingers possessed a venom that neutralized the Arachnid's toxins.

Selma lowered her chin.

With the poison neutralized, she initiated the healing component. She cupped her hands around her mouth and allowed her breath to warm her palms. She placed her hands on the boy's heart and began to hum.

"Antala-wa-shay ... Onnn-ta-laaa-wa-sheee ..."

The vibrations caused the bees to fall from the boy's head. She continued until the boy's internal frequency aligned with her own. Once their frequencies synced, she crescendoed the vibrations until the boy's cells awakened. At that point, she spoke to each cell, empowering them. Each cell listened, awakened, and regenerated itself.

She removed her hands from the boy, stepped back, and allowed the boy space.

Antiochticus slowly regained himself. First, he regained control of his mind. Followed by the function of his body. He coughed twice and slowly opened his eyes. A thick-black substance spilled from his mouth.

This was his first time having a clear look at Selma. He had sensed her presence and felt no fear, but looking upon her evoked a different sentiment. She was extremely tall. He had never seen a Myer Ram, and she was daunting. The only concept he had was from his mother's fairy tales.

"Arise child. Come," said Selma.

Selma cut the boy's spectacle short, not allowing him time to ask questions. She summoned a portal and motioned the boy to follow as she stepped through. He hesitated before following.

❦ ❦

Selma stood over an open flame within her quaint and cozy den preparing soup. Her favorite color, orange, was a central theme of the den. Carved wooden hands, claws, and hoofs of all species, shapes, sizes, and colors were mounted throughout the den. Upon the walls were paintings Selma had produced.

Antiochticus sat on one of the den's rugs, gazing in astonishment. He hadn't been in a home in quite a while. Constantly on the run, his mother was never able to settle. She did her best to make a home out of every place they laid their heads at night.

The boy was like a refugee in many ways—dogmatic persecution forced his mother to flee their tribe. The only dogma he adhered to was 'trust no one,' and his Holy Land was the Abyss where he sought to reunite with his mother.

The den resided inside the trunk of a tree three times the size of a redwood. It consisted of four rooms, each fulfilling a unique purpose. The room they were currently in contained a large black cooking pot, two rocking chairs, and an open space to dine. The child wondered why there was a second rocking chair.

He patiently waited for Selma to finish cooking. The scent of cinnamon overpowered all other smells. He didn't feel odd, or on edge, surprisingly, he felt a level of comfort as his eyes transfixed on the titillating shades of orange that decorated the room.

Selma served the child, and she sat in the larger rocking chair. Antiochticus sat at her feet and reached for the bowl.

"Be careful with that. It's still hot."

He put the bowl to his mouth and slurped.

Selma observed and didn't judge him for his lack of etiquette but took note. "No, no, no, here," she levitated the spoon towards him, "use this."

He grabbed the spoon and held it firmly. Having been on the run, he had never been afforded the luxury of using utensils.

"You don't have to use it if you don't want to. It's okay," reassured Selma. Her curiosity was peaked. He has no shame of social manners; he's been apart from society for quite some time. She thought. "How'd did you find yourself out here child? The nearest village is eighteen days' journey away, and you made it this far by your lonely? What tribe are you?"

Antiochticus slurped from the bowl without bothering to wipe his mouth. In between slurps, he replied, "I have no tribe. I'm going to the Abyss."

Selma chuckled slightly.

"Don't be foolish, child. There is no such place. Besides, everyone has a tribe, child. What tribe did you come from?"

Selma saw the boy's face tense. He inhaled a deep breath filled with despair and gently placed his bowl of soup on the floor in front of him. He turned his face from Selma. Selma realized the boy had very little trust for anyone. She sensed he'd been through much scarring in his short lifetime—pain and ambition fueled him.

"May I share a story with you?" asked Selma.

She opened her mind and invited the boy within her thoughts. With supreme control of her mind, she had adroitly compartmentalized her memories. She created a bridge within her thoughts and urged Antiochticus to cross. He found himself outside of his mind, yet still within his body. He felt ethereal, as though he was without mass. It was almost as though he was a spectator of a dream— someone else's dream. The tension and coldness of the air gave him goosebumps.

Selma's memory began at the edge of a wooden bridge. Antiochticus approached the bridge, halted near the middle, and looked down into an endless abyss. He knew it wasn't 'the Abyss,' but wondered how much they had in common. He continued along the bridge, and his eyes widened as he recognized Selma standing on the other side. She appeared much different. She was stout, robust, and her fleshy limbs were covered in illustrious brown earth-toned fur. She was youthful.

Being reduced to a quiet observer, he could not interact with her. The memory progressed quickly, and he noticed Selma was the object-of-desire of every male Myer Ram.

She maneuvered through the herd with a regal bearing, its King was a ram named Denascus. He announced an edict that would make Selma his newest Queen. The ceremony would last seven moons. All was well, until Leopold, Denascus's eldest son, assaulted her on the fifth moon. She successfully fended him off but did not disclose the assault to the King. On the night of the seventh moon, the ceremony culminated with Selma receiving the amulet. It was an amulet with a blue and green beetle shaped jewel as the centerpiece.

Antiochticus stared at the beetle as it rested on Selma's chest. The memory suspended as Antiochticus' gaze transfixed upon the beetle. It began to hum, and slowly lifted one leg at a time until it detached from the amulet. Antiochticus titled his head in curiosity as the beetle seemed to be flying towards him. He moved his head to avoid the beetle as it whizzed by. It circled back around and landed on his forehead. He stood perfectly still. The beetle flapped its wings and time seemed to slow because

Antiochticus could feel each vibration of the beetle's wings penetrate his mind.

Selma's memory suddenly resumed, and he couldn't discern if what he experienced actually happened or not.

Leopold and his mother, Mya, conspired to murder Denascus, and Selma was to be the scapegoat. They succeeded, and Selma was beaten and condemned to death for her transgression. As the new King, Leopold pardoned her on the condition that she give herself to him unconditionally and provide penance for her wrongdoing. She accepted the offer, but used the opportunity to craft an escape—a death sentence in itself, because no Myer Ram had ever survived without the herd.

The memory ended abruptly, and Antiochticus began shivering from the cold. The vengeance harbored from the memory inundated the atmosphere and created a viscosity. He struggled with each step to return to the bridge. The atmosphere was so thick that each step felt like he was marching through quicksand.

After crossing the bridge, Antiochticus was back within himself—sitting on the carpet at the feet of Selma. He felt a compelling compassion because the memory resonated with his spirit. He looked down at his arm and saw goosebumps that displayed the residual of Selma's pain. He felt that Selma and he were alike—in the sense that vengeance burned through their soul like a fire to a wick. Memories of his mother flooded Antiochticus' mind. Thoughts regarding her—a joy that he was now deprived of—inevitably turned him ice cold.

"Selma, I can see me in you. And it makes me sad."

"Child … do not waste your emotion. It will not change anything. It will only fuel your undoing," replied Selma.

The two remained still in an uncomfortable silence. Selma looked off into the distance.

"I am looking for my destiny in the happy place. I need to find the Abyss. Will you help me?" Antiochticus spoke with an unrelenting determination, yet he understood he was indebted to Selma.

"I've helped you, and I will continue to help you, but I desire help as well. Perhaps we may kill two birds with one destiny," she replied.

The boy tilted his head all the way back, enabling him to look into Selma's face. He felt obliged and was eager to please.

"Anti, do you understand the difference between Justice and Vengeance?"

A cold shiver rushed across Anti as his goosebumps tingled. His eyes shifted up and to the left, as he thought about how his mom used to call him Anti. He didn't seek to correct Selma because hearing her call him that felt natural. He recognized the thin line between justice and vengeance but was curious as to the answer Selma would provide. He locked eyes with her and shook his head from side to side.

"Life will give you unique experiences that will provide you with cruel awakenings. Vengeance is but for personal gain. Justice sets the universe back on its proper course—it restores order."

Anti ingested the axiom.

"I seek both vengeance and justice, Anti. By saving you, I have lost my amulet. It enhances who I am. It acts as a spotlight unto my soul—illuminating my destiny in the process. The amulet is but one piece of a whole provided to me as a gift the night I was to consummate my queen-ship. I would like the other part of that whole Anti. This will clear your debt, and in turn, help you discover who you are."

Anti sat pensively at the ram's feet. He had no idea how to attain the amulet. He had no idea the power the amulet possessed, and he had no idea what means he would have to utilize to attain the amulet. He was young but full of boundless courage. Anti had been through so much in his short lifetime. This was but another straw to add to the stack. He just hoped it wasn't the straw that would break the camel's back.

He stood to his feet and reached for Selma's palms.

"I will, and I am forever within your debt. Your misery is my cup to bare," said Anti.

"I have faith you will succeed. Be careful, the power of the amulet expresses itself in different ways to its owner. The wearer of it, will not give it up without a fight."

Anti understood the words between the words. He was a boy, yet he possessed ageless wisdom. He did not know how to harness this wisdom in its totality. He released his grasp of her hands and stepped back.

"The Abyss is my destiny, Selma. I'm sure of this. You and your magic have assured me of this."

"Your destiny will always be. Do not allow dreams to curve your reality."

Anti tilted his head downward.

"I will retrieve your amulet. Will you then show me the way to the Abyss?"

"When you retrieve the amulet; you will know the way to the Abyss. I've never seen it, to me it does not exist, but it isn't meant to exist for me."

Anti thought about Selma's last statement. He didn't know how to digest it. He trusted Selma because he understood her pain.

"Finish your soup, Anti."

"You know, all who have ever loved me have called me Anti," he said coyly. Selma thought about the implications of the statement, and her soul began to warm. She kept her silence as the boy finished his soup.

"Come, you must rest. You are not yet ready for your journey. You still need knowledge. Let me prepare you," Selma requested after Anti finished his meal.

Selma lead the boy to a different room. It was completely dark and devoid of scent. It contained a slab of stone within the middle that enhanced the room's aura. She directed the boy to lay atop the stone. The cold tensed his flesh.

She chanted, "Umbalaca ... um-ba ... uummm ... bbaaa ... unba-laaa-caaa ... laca ... ummm."

The incantation's effects weren't evident but were completely necessary for Anti to survive the journey.

Selma's compassion reminded him of his mother and his eyes watered. He slowly sunk within himself as the chanting continued. Anti descended for quite some time, yet to him, it felt like a dream. He awoke to see Selma painting in the corner. The room was now filled with bright light.

"Here, put this on, Anti." Selma handed him a burnt orange woven trouser and shirt. "I've prepared for you a final meal and sack for you to take on your quest."

"Do you think, I'm ready?"

"I'm sure you are," Selma calmly replied.

"But there's so much magic out there, and I know none."

"Oh," Selma replied with a skeptical tone. Anti squinted his eyebrows in bemusement. "Then what's that in your pocket?"

He patted the sides of his pants. Then reached inside of his pocket and felt the flutter of insect wings. As he withdrew his hand, the insect snuggled firmly into his palm. When he opened his palm, he was astonished to see the very same beetle from Selma's memory.

"What—but how?"

"Magic isn't something that can be taught or passed down, Anti. It isn't a skill that can be developed. It is knowledge that some innately have. The process of learning magic is the process of self-discovery and self-realization of that which is already in you," she said.

While examining the beetle within his palm, it seemingly vanished.

"It's something you step into; if the mind could understand, then it wouldn't be magic. It's a feeling, like when you instinctively know something has been staring at you, it's that exact feeling but amplified a hundredfold. Yet, it is quite fragile as well, one falter of faith and the entire system crumbles."

Anti followed Selma as she exited the room. She handed him the sack which contained snacks and other essentials.

"Be careful, on your journey to the Myer camp there will be many obstacles. The most powerful of which will be the

Sebastian Serpent." She bent down so that she was eye level with Anti. She looked directly into his eyes and continued to speak, "She is an extremely dangerous viper. She appears harmless, but her bite is vicious."

She simultaneously rubbed the forehead and upper chest of Anti. He shivered at her touch and felt a jolt of energy pulsate throughout his body. "She feeds off of memories. She can draw you so far within yourself that you may find yourself unable to escape. You and your memories become hers to harvest forever as an energy source. She lives off the minds of many. Avoid the serpent at all cost."

Anti didn't realize Selma was providing him with the Myer Ram scent. Scent was the Myer Ram's primary means of communication. They could pick up a scent from up to fifty miles away, and it would alert the herd to any potential threat. This would allow the boy some advantage in approaching the camp, but once confronted by a Myer lookout, the rest would be up to him.

Anti's body and mind were properly prepared. Selma knew the boy possessed great willpower and was confident that his willpower, alone, would be the guiding light and anchor of his excursion. Before she let Anti leave, she informed him that an invisibility potion was inside of his sack and provided instructions for usage. She explained that it would be a vital resource for his campaign to obtain the amulet. Selma created a portal for Anti that would lead him to the edge of the forest. He was hesitant before walking through and wondered if he would see Selma again. He looked back towards her before proceeding, she felt a slight shame and hid her face.

꙳ ꙳

"I don't know how this will go. Mom, I know you're out there somewhere, I could really use your help. I don't know if I will be able to do this alone, but if it eventually brings me closer to you, I will try my best. I met a lady who reminded me a lot of you. She says she'll help me find you and I believe her. It won't be long, Mom. I promise.

I feel like there's so much magic out there that is just waiting to be seized—some of it good, some of it bad. I don't even know if it's meant for me. All that I know is that I am meant for the Abyss. I've never felt like you've ever left me. I can see you when I sleep, but like now, I always feel you when I'm awake. I never feel alone, that's the only reason that I feel what I'm doing is right. You're my sight when I can't see."

Several days into his journey, Anti had yet to show signs of fatigue. He remained in high spirits. The time spent with his mother on the run had allowed him to adeptly adapt to survival. Magic accentuated that skill. Confidence in his abilities grew as his level of understanding encouraged him to delve deeper into the craft. He noticed when the beetle appeared, his abilities tended to manifest more fluently but didn't quite understand the connection.

One afternoon, as the sun set, he discovered the pack that Selma prepared had depleted of snacks, so he devised a plan to find food. He heard the roar of the Mystique River nearby as he entered Shallow Hearts Jungle, which was full of Goiya trees. He had only tasted the fruit of a Gioya tree once when his mother was able to distract a Merskaw. Since the shell of the fruit was so hard, only the claws of a Merskaw could pry open the robust, pink fruit.

As Anti traveled deeper into Shallow Hearts Jungle, he heard the caws of several Merkshaws in the distance. He saw a few jumping from tree to tree in a monkey-like fashion. Anti recalled his mother's words, "No Anti, they aren't monkeys. They are Mershaw, they have long tails just like monkeys, but they only have one eye and their fur is always black." Although their caws were intimidating and high pitched, Anti had no fear of the creatures because of their non-threatening nature.

Anti saw several large Goiya trees in the distance. Resembling large palm trees, he knew there would be no way he could reach the fruit without help. He needed help from the Merkshaw, but they weren't motivated by much outside of the fruit— except for shiny things.

As he approached the Goiya tree, he saw two small Merskaw lounging. He couldn't discern if they were sleeping and attempted to shake the base of the tree to gather their attention, but the tree didn't budge. He attempted to will the fruit down with his mind, in a different approach, but that didn't work.

He sat at the base of the tree and sighed. He was alerted by a buzzing sound inside of his pocket. Reaching inside, he felt a beetle's wings flutter eagerly. When he withdrew the beetle, he noticed its color changed. It now possessed the radiance of a shiny silver hue. It tickled as it climbed up his arm, making its way up his neck, pausing on his nose to flutter.

The beetle flew towards the Merskaws. Their eye's bulged and they almost fell from the tree reaching for it. Despite their friendly demeanor, they aggressively wrestled each other for the beetle's possession and fell from the tree in the process, landing with a thud. The chubbier one broke the fall of the other. The taller Merskaw sprung up unscathed, looked down at his partner and continued to climb the tree. He showed no concern as his partner remained motionless. He climbed with a feverish relentlessness in pursuit of the beetle.

Anti shielded his eyes from the beetle's glimmer as he stood at the base of the tree. The Merskaw reached for the beetle, but it flew atop a Goiya and escaped his efforts. He reached again but failed as the beetle sunk into the Goiya fruit. He grabbed the fruit and feverishly clawed at the shell, slicing it open until he was tackled from behind. The shorter-chubby Merskaw had awakened and attacked his partner. Both, along with the fruit, fell from the tree. They popped right up and quarreled while the beetle emerged and flew off into the jungle. The two paused before ferociously taking off in pursuit.

Anti reached down to pick up the fruit and felt a vibration in his pocket. He paused, *Am I controlling the beetle or is it controlling itself?* The thought was fleeting, but the satiation of the Goiya fruit was lasting.

He ate until he was full and placed the remainder in his sack. He traversed further into the jungle until he reached the Mystique River. He recalled Selma's advice, "The river will cut several days from your journey, but you run the greater risk of running into the Sebastian Serpent." Anti possessed an innate ability to deter fear, or he was too brazen for his own good. Most of his journey so far had been through desert terrain until he reached the jungle.

The time that Anti spent with Selma, preparing for the journey, allowed him to develop a certain level of comfort with the magic that ubiquitously surrounded him.

Selma had stated, "Magic is nothing more than energy— few can see it and even fewer can harness it. Magic can be amplified and guided, but never created or stored. Like light, it has a very large spectrum—much like light, individuals are limited by how much they can perceive. You must open your eyes, Anti. This is what allows different individuals to express magic in different manners."

At night, near the river, he and the beetle prepared a fire to keep warm—his desire to keep warm seamlessly manifested. This taught him magic was a phenomenon of the imagination.

Anti recalled Selma saying, "Remember Anti, magic is not an objective force to be acted upon, on the contrary, magic itself is always an active participant in the process. It chooses to show itself differently to different people. It has a way of humbling you and balancing things."

The river's roar was daunting. He felt it was taunting him, daring him to enter. Anti approached the river, placed his hand in the water, and allowed it to rage by. He closed his eyes and tried his best to manifest a raft, but fear and doubt inhibited his abilities. He opened his eyes, stepped back, and took a deep breath. When he opened his eyes again, he saw the beetle flying in a spiral motion to his right, and from thin air, a yellow energy field emerged and transformed into a raft. After he climbed on top, the beetle propelled it into the water.

He struggled to balance atop the raft while the river whipped and roared creating a tumultuous ride. The river gradually calmed, and the air grew thick and humid; beads of sweat began to stream down Anti's face. After a while, he grew tired, dozed off, and his mind began to dream.

Anti's body convulsed in a cold shiver as he heard a quiet whisper.

"I can show you your heart's desire."

Startled by the voice, Anti awoke in a panic. All signs lead him to believe he was awake. The smooth pace of the river had now become tumultuous again. The atmosphere was so dark that Anti couldn't see his hand as he waved it in front of his face.

"Can you distinguish the real from the unreal?" whispered the voice.

Anti frantically searched the darkness and shouted, "Show yourself! Who's there?" He had used Selma's sack as a pillow while he rested. In a panic, he searched for it as the river's torrent increased. He blindly reached but could feel nothing. *I need that potion*, thought Anti, *how else will I be able to sneak into the Myer Camp?*

"Shhh ... If you really want to see me, quiet your mind. You think with too much emotion," responded the voice.

Anti wasn't sure what to do. He felt despair as the possibility of losing the potion sunk in. He felt as though the river was taunting him, and his weakened state of mind started affecting the rafts composition.

"Shhh ... You're losing a hold of yourself. It's all falling apart ..."

The voice agitated Anti, but his concern for the river was more pressing. He tried to grab hold of the raft to brace himself, but as he reached there was nothing for him to grab. His heartbeat quickened. *What happened?* Anti thought.

"Shhh, relax. I can save you. Do you want to be saved?" asked the voice. She spoke with an enticing whisper.

Anti spit out mouthfuls of water as he smacked the icy river. He struggled with its current, flailing his arms in an attempt to keep his head above water. The river was swallowing him, and it had a long list of victims. Anti fought to keep his name off of that list.

"Shhh ... quiet your mind child, panic will only ensure your demise. Follow my words. Do you see them?" asked the voice.

Anti coughed up water as his head ebbed below the surface of the water and back up. From the corner of his eye, he could see a very bright golden glow within the water.

"Aww ... you can see it now. I will save you, child. My name is Victoria. You only need to keep a quiet mind and visualize the words I speak. Let my words in, and I will save you," whispered Victoria.

He stopped fighting. His body was too fatigued to stay afloat, he felt himself submerging until he became engulfed within the golden glow. It elevated his body. He allowed Victoria's words to seize hold of his mind, and as he did, the darkness lifted, the river stopped fighting, and his body floated without any effort of its own.

"Shhh ... Now stand and walk on top of my words."

He followed her instructions, wobbling a bit while slowly allowing her words to stabilize his footing. The golden glow hardened into floating stepping-stones, creating a trail leading to the river bank. Anti hesitated before exiting the river, he did not want to detour his journey but felt he had no other choice.

"Shhh ... You possess immense power, boy. But it's trapped within. I can free you. Follow me."

Anti followed the golden path through the darkness. He saw little, but the glow of her words illuminated his way. His fingertips felt numb, and the cold intensified with each step. It didn't take long for his teeth to begin chattering.

"Shhh ... quiet your mind, the cold is but the weakness of your thoughts. Empty your thoughts, and I can remove all obstructions to power."

He no longer felt his hands or toes. The more he allowed Victoria within his thoughts, the colder it became. The darkness slowly lifted, and he found himself in the middle of a large field of ice in the midst of a snowstorm. He was unable to feel due to the onset of hypothermia.

He faintly heard Victoria as though she was a long distance away. The atmosphere brightened, Anti saw an igloo a few hundred yards away, and it appeared to be the source of her voice.

"What's your truth? Can you rewrite history within yourself? If you change what you remember, then the truth becomes what you make it. I can teach you the science of truth. Follow me ..." she insisted.

He entered the igloo and collapsed. He felt relief from the igloo's warmth. He lay motionless, with his eyes closed, until the blood returned to his frostbitten limbs. After opening his eyes, he was finally able to see the source of the words.

His eyes watered as he witnessed his mother sitting cross-legged.

"Mom!?!" he shouted, "but I thought you were—" he was too weakened to rise, and remained face down on a grey rug.

"Alive!!" interrupted his mother, "I am very much alive, Anti. I've always been, I've just been waiting for you, and now you're here. I'm just so happy to see you."

A solitary tear streamed down his face. "But you were supposed to be at the Abyss ... the happy place ..." He felt discomfort. Something about her kept him cautious. He didn't yearn for her touch. He saw his mother die and this wasn't who he saw, "but where are your scars?" he asked.

She leaned down and kissed his forehead. He felt her warm embrace as she whispered, "Memories aren't memories as we would like them to be. Memories are realities that live on forever and create a life of their own. I've remained in your mind, safe and sound from any harm. You have saved me, Anti."

He very much missed his mother and couldn't help but to relish her clasp. It reminded him of his mother, from the touch down to her scent of rosemary.

"Mama, do you remember the story of my birth?"

"Of course. How could I forget?"

He quickly lost himself within the memory. The story had been told to him so often that the memory felt true. He saw his mother go into labor and give birth under the solace of a clear night sky. He saw three northern stars perfectly aligned. He saw a young woman, alone, afraid, and holding a child not knowing what to do next. So many questions flooded his mind. *Why was she alone? Why didn't I have a tribal birth? Why was she scared?*

He noticed something about the memory that he hadn't before. There were three owls flying in a circle above him and his mother. He heard voices in the distance. His mother had never told him about this part of the story.

"She's over here!" exclaimed one of the men. "Did you really think we wouldn't find you." She clutched her newborn tightly and refused to respond. "You really believed you could escape the Republic, didn't you? You are among the condemned, and no matter how far you run, we will find you."

Four men wearing combat attire surrounded her. They wore helmets of bronze with the insignia of a scorpion, leather breastplates, and had swords and shields of steel.

"No!" she cried out.

"Quiet Sorren! Accept fate and hand over the child," said one of the men. The voice belonged to a man she had once adored. A man who she desperately wanted Anti to grow up knowing as his father, but due to circumstance, she feared would never be the case. "We've discussed this. The boy is a threat to the Republic, he's an abomination that will bring forth nothing but pain and destruction upon the earth, as the prophecy stated. I've accepted this, why can't you. He's my flesh and blood just as he is yours, you can't run forever."

She had no intention of relinquishing her newborn— instinct would not allow her to.

"Just because these men have conquered our tribe and forced their beliefs upon us, doesn't mean I have to accept it," she pleaded, hoping her lover would choose his family over the fear he had of his conquerors.

"Sorren, listen, there is nothing we can do. Just give up the child," his father spoke with great regret because he knew he was taking the easiest way out. The father had thought to himself, "How could a man ask his child to lay down his life?"

As the other three soldiers approached Sorren with swords drawn, she screamed at the top of her lungs. While doing so, the owls hovering above joined in and shrieked in unison. The piercing sound caused the soldiers to drop to their knees in agony. The loud pitch caused a rift that created a portal allowing dozens of beetles to fly out.

Anti interrupted the memory. "No this isn't right!" tears flowed as he lay face down. Sorren slowly rubbed his back. "You always told me that one of the four pursuers was my father. You told me that he sacrificed his life for mine, and he would not let any of the other pursuers harm me. You said, he died from a mortal wound and was able to hold me in his arms as his final living act," cried Anti.

"Shhh," replied Sorren, "that's the beauty of rewriting history. It's how I am alive this day, Anti. How can a memory you just envisioned, be a lie? Do you believe the memory possessed a life of its own and decided to deviate from the truth? Quiet your thoughts and open your mind, let mama help you," she said softly. She relinquished him, stepped back, and looked into his eyes as he lay face down. His body felt cold again. In his pocket, he felt a vibration followed by a tiny pinch. He didn't wince from the pain, but his entire body began to convulse.

"You're not my mother!" Anti chanted over and over at as loud of a decibel as he could. "You're not my mother!" He regained his strength with each utterance of the affirmation. "You're not my mother!" He stood to his feet fully invigorated. "Who are you!"

The woman matched his defiant posture. "I can be whatever you like. Whom do you hold of more value than mommy-dearest?"

He felt provoked and began to fill with anger. *Where am I? What am I doing here? Who is this woman and what does she want from me?*

Victoria realized she was losing control of Anti's mind. She was powerless if she could not remain hidden within his mind.

As Anti looked into Sorren's eyes, her image began to flicker in and out. He noticed Sorren wasn't the only thing fading in and out, everything began to flicker, the rug he was standing on, the igloo, the snowstorm, all of it. He closed his eyes in anticipation that he too might disappear.

Slowly opening his eyes, he recognized he was still on the river, laying on top of the raft. He raised himself to a seated position and elongated his breathing. He looked around for some type of explanation but noticed nothing outside of the ordinary except a diminutive serpent on the edge of the raft.

The serpent was about the size of his ring finger. She hissed and attempted to strike a beetle that hovered above it. Anti regained his bearings and swatted her into the river. As he did so, Victoria managed to snag his finger and inflict a small dosage of venom. The effects were minimal. He still had neutralizing agents from the unseen honey bees of Galoria running through his blood.

⚘ ⚘

Anti remained steadfast in his journey. He no longer missed his mother in the same way. He knew, despite any memory of her, she lived in peace within his heart, and that when he reached the Abyss, he would see her again. The Myer Ram camp was drawing near.

When he lost Selma's sack in the river, he lost the invisibility potion and along with it his plan to obtain the amulet. He had grown quite comfortable with his abilities and knowledge thus far and felt the beetle would somehow help him retrieve the amulet.

As he drew closer to the camp, the landscape transformed. It resembled the fairy tales that his mother had told each night while rocking him to sleep. The luscious grassland possessed blades as tall as his waist with a bright hue.

The nomadic rams tended to migrate cyclically and remained within a fifty-mile radius. They preferred valleys due to their strategical makeup; it allowed them to see and hear impending intruders with ease, and they could easily drink from rivers that ran near the base.

Anti decided to approach the camp during the day. As the sun set, he made rest for the night. The beetle combusted, creating a small fire. Anti wondered if he could levitate and hover above the flames. As the thought resonated, his body slowly elevated. He leaned back until he became parallel and suspended supine in the air. While floating above the small flame, he closed his eyes.

"Put your magic away immediately!" a voice commanded with authority.

Anti landed with a thump and rolled away from the fire. The bass from the voice vibrated his insides. *What? Who?* he thought.

He opened his eyes and found himself face to face with two, gargantuan Myer Ram. They were more daunting than he anticipated, appearing twice the size of Selma, possessing bolstering horns. Both were covered from head to toe with brown woolly fur. Their eyes were bold, menacing, with a yellowish tinge. Anti felt the potential power their muscles harnessed, just from their mere presence.

But how did they sneak up on me? Anti had no time to think. He scrambled to compose his thoughts and nerves.

"State your presence!" commanded the bulkier ram.

Anti stumbled to his feet, responding meekly, "I ... I ... I am Antiochticus. And I come in peace." He had never felt that level of fear. He did not know it could be that gripping.

He looked up to see the ram's yellow eyes piercing through the darkness. He noticed the ram wasn't so much looking at him but towards him. He figured they didn't possess the best eyesight—and this was true. They saw great from long distances but anything directly in front of them became an indistinguishable blur. The fact that Selma made his scent compatible with the Ram's lead him to further believe that they relied heavily upon smell. He knew he had to use this to his advantage.

"This way! The King will decide what to do with you, intruder!"

The rams led him through the night, across the Myer's camp. Despite the darkness, Anti was in awe. The ostentation and size of the Myer's tents weakened his knees; massive teepees made from the hide of Slanghals—colossal beasts who were considered sacred by the Myer Ram. Small fires provided illumination throughout the camp. He spotted what had to be the King's tent immediately. It was much larger than any other tent with a giant totem pole situated in front.

Along the walls of the crown ram's tent were the heads of different species, many of which Anti had never seen before—horns, snouts, and teeth. Weapons of war were situated along the room, and it appeared red and purple were his favorite colors because that seemed to be the motif.

Anti was thrown at the King's hooves atop a red velvet, fur-like rug. The king's size made the two scout rams look like adolescents. His black wool possessed a sheen. He wore an amulet around his neck and a golden shield across his left shoulder. His horns were thick, and the tips had a gold covering. He represented the epitome of an alpha-male, in form if not also function.

He wore the amulet with great pride and regal bearing. It refracted light brilliantly—Anti shielded his eyes from the glare.

Anti slowly stumbled to his feet. The King snorted and sniffed profusely.

"The intruder, your Majesty," the scout proclaimed while keeping his head bowed and eyes averted. He didn't dare look into the King's face.

The King looked toward Anti but never directly at him, more so through him.

"He is of no threat! His nuts have yet to descend. What is your tribe, kid?" commanded the King.

The King had yet to discern that Anti was human, Selma had pulled through, but Anti wasn't sure how long the scent would last. Anti claimed no tribe, even if he could lie, he wouldn't have known what lie to tell.

"I have no tribe, sir," he retorted.

"The insolence of this kid! How dare you speak in the presence of a King. Blasphemy! On top of that, you lie! No one survives without their tribe! Who sent you and why? Are you some type of mercenary? Choose your next response wisely."

Anti trembled. The King spoke with so much bass that it knocked Anti's feet out from under him. He frantically picked himself back up, and wanted very much to use magic in the situation but thought better of it.

"I've come for your amulet, oh gracious King."

"My amulet?" The king retorted with immense sarcasm. The King broke out in booming laughter. The scouts joined in the amusement.

"Silence!" commanded the King.

Everyone's attention shifted to the rear of the tent. A smaller ram emerged from a partition. She was Selma's size and possessed salt and pepper sprinkled white wool. It covered her entire body. She had short, stubby horns that were rounded off. Between her horns rested a purple, fez-shaped cap. She wore a purple, V-shaped garment across her torso.

Gracefully, she glided across the room, and as Anti took a double take, he realized her hooves were elevated, and she was floating. She didn't bother to look in Anti's direction as she approached the King. She placed her hand on top of his massive hand, and she conferred with him in a whisper.

"My Queen, what do you suggest we do with the boy. He's clearly a spy sent to see how powerful of a defense we can muster. I just can't understand why the Republic would dare send a boy," said the King.

"Leopold, do not be foolish. He is telling the truth. He was not sent by the Republic. He isn't even a ram. He's a human."

"Mother, am I the one being foolish here?"

"How dare you? Check your impudence!"

"I'm sorry my Queen, but Mom. It's just, a human has never made it this far. Could this be some trick by the Republic?"

"I do not know, Leopold. I do not have a good feeling about him. I suggest you eliminate the threat immediately!"

"Threat?" questioned Leopold. He shifted on his throne and lifted his chin.

Leopold stood and approached Anti. He bent down and pressed his snout directly against Anti's chest and sniffed profusely, his entire body—front to back, top to bottom. He stepped back and summoned for his advisor.

"Summon the herd, tomorrow morning an official edict must be made. I need to address our intruder."

The three suns illuminated the entire camp the following morning. Leopold stood on a large mound of grass in front of the herd with Anti by his left side and his mother to the rear. The crowd seemed like an endless sea of mass to Anti. He shielded his eyes from the suns' brightness. He had butterflies in his stomach and didn't know what to expect or what he should do. The crowd's clamor vibrated the mound. A loud horn sounded and everyone silenced. Anti stretched his neck to look up at Leopold as he addressed the multitude.

"I know many of you have been on edge lately, ever since we have gotten word of the Republic's intention of expansion and their impending advances. It isn't a matter of when they will attack, but how. As you are well aware, we have increased our scout team, so an attack should not be a surprise. As some of you may have already heard, we captured an intruder last night."

Anti fidgeted as the herd murmured. He stood awkwardly with his legs crossed.

"We don't believe he is connected in any way to the Republic."

Leopold stomped his hooves incessantly. It created a thunderous crescendo. Anti stumbled but quickly regained his composure. Leopold abruptly stopped, shifted his demeanor, and hollowed his tone to a bellow.

"SO THE BOY WANTS THE AMULET!"

The crowd grumbled.

"YOU HEARD ME CORRECTLY, AN INTRUDER CHALLENGES FOR THE THRONE—A HUMAN BOY AT THAT!" the king stomped his hooves. He pivoted in a circle three times while rhythmically stamping his feet. He snorted and roared, performing the ritualistic King's rebuttal. The dance solidified his acceptance of the Duel for Supremacy.

Any time a king was challenged for the throne in an open forum, he had to accept to avoid appearing weak. It's to the death, so the challenge rarely occurred. Leopold had never been challenged. No one was foolish enough to challenge a King, especially since the King wore an amulet that enhanced his power disproportionately. No one dared combat the amulet's power.

"LET THE FESTIVITIES BEGIN!"

The herd unanimously erupted, with the exception of Leopold's mother.

"Fool," she muttered sternly under her breath.

"HE HAS UNTIL THE NEXT DEAD MOONS TO PREPARE HIMSELF!"

Leopold bent down and whispered, "What is your name, boy?"

"Antiochticus."

Leopold stepped back to readdress the multitude.

"IN THE MEANTIME, TREAT ANTIOCHTICUS AS YOU WOULD MYSELF! A ROUND OF APPLAUSE FOR OUR GUEST OF HONOR!!"

🌿 🌿

Anti quickly discerned he was in over his head—a boy sent to do a man's job. The Myer Rams were a warlike bunch, yet relied heavily upon spiritual customs. They did not have a specific religion or deity, for there was no religion of the land, but they did follow strict spiritual protocol provided by the herd spiritualist. In this instance, the spiritualist was Leopold's mother, Mya. She warned her son of the impending danger the boy possessed. Leopold did not perceive the threat because he lived in an environment where magic was prohibited.

He understood power from a limited perspective and didn't see the big picture—a character trait Mya disdained about her son. The only magic Leopold and the herd were exposed to were the powers of the amulet, and they believed that was merely an instrument of a mysterious higher source, not something they each had a power to tap into. Mya, on the contrary, was well aware of the magic realm and hid the knowledge as a means of control and fear.

Anti had until the dead moons to live among them before the ceremonial fight-to-the-death commenced. This allowed him plenty of time to adjust to their customs and live among them as their own.

Anti enjoyed the time spent with the herd and developed a large level of comfort. Each morning he traversed with the worker rams to gather fresh water. He enjoyed this time because there was a science to locating the freshest watering holes and a peacefulness to it—sensing nature's milk and honey. He learned that duties were shared and rotated cyclically.

Anti had been exiled by his tribe and enjoyed the feeling of being accepted. He was treated as the King was, but unlike the King, he was a humble ruler—never asking for more than was necessary. Anti was extremely polite and spent most of his time observing.

He spent the majority of his nights in trepidation, the truth was, he did not know how he would defeat Leopold. Anti spent his time training alone—meditating and covertly practicing magic. If the fight came down to a battle of brute force, he stood no chance; and if he utilized overt magic, he would be put to death due to its prohibition. His only hope was to attack the mind of the great beast.

He practiced the techniques learned from his experience with Victoria. She was able to sneak into Anti's mind and wreak havoc, and he intended to utilize the same tactics. He would have to gradually possess the beast's mind. He couldn't wait until the day of the event, he had to begin the process early.

The King slept separately from the rest of the herd; this provided the advantage Anti needed. Every night he entered Leopold's mind via his dreams. After several nights, Leopold grew comfortable with the invader that harbored within his mind. In fact, Leopold developed a cognitive dissonance. Anti presented himself as Leopold's father within each dream. He focused on the part of Leopold's mind that remained dormant, compartmental-ized, and repressed.

He brought these dormant memories to the forefront of Leopold's mind. The more Leopold dreamed of the father he murdered, the more his conscious dissociation solidified.

Night after night, Anti's presence within Leopold's mind strengthened. He eventually rewrote Leopold's truth by reconstructing the memory of his father's murder. He showed Leopold his father's anabiosis. Subconsciously, Leopold was convinced his father still lived, and his guilt was forcing him to pay a penance for his treachery. Anti had the king's mind booby-trapped. He put triggers in place that enabled him to attack the conscious mind when the time was right. It allowed the subconscious reality to flood his mind and it would become truth at the perfect waking moment.

Within several nights, Anti supplanted the memory of Leopold's father, Denascus, and replaced it with himself. He became Denascus. He was Denascus.

※ ※

One night, while Anti explored Leopold's dreams, his pocket began to vibrate. He was surprised because the beetle had been absent since he had reached the Myer camp. He felt his heartbeat quicken and opened his eyes, but before he could reach into his pocket, he found himself involuntarily standing to his feet. He had lost control of all faculties except his head and neck, which he could freely move. His body began walking and, to his left, saw Leopold exiting the King's chamber.

The fear was suffocating, and Anti wanted to cry out, but couldn't. He could only blink and look around. The moonlit sky illuminated the camp. Befuddled, Anti witnessed ram after ram marching in single file lines towards the mound. He saw a burning cross in the distance with a plague of locust hovering above it.

His stomach churned. Powerless, he was unable to break free from the herd's hypnotizing march. Fear enveloped the faces of his peers, and he wondered whose control they were under.

Gradually, they settled in front of the burning cross situated on the same mound Leopold had used to address the herd. Anti was too far away to see what was on the cross.

He felt his pocket vibrate and shuddered as the beetle crawled out of his pocket, along his spine, stopping to rest near the base of his skull. Its wings fluttered, and Anti slowly wiggled his fingers and bent his knees.

Anti stealthily maneuvered through the stone-like rams until he reached the front. His eyes blossomed as he witnessed Leopold on bended knee, hands to the sky, at the base of the mound.

Anti's heartbeat quickened as he looked upon the massive cross—its edges ablaze.

Mounted on top of the burning cross was the Queen. Her horns severed—nothing remaining except sawed off nubs. Mya was centered, head sunken, unable to free herself with a black ooze dripping from her nubs. A plague of locust flew above her head. Anti shielded his ears from the buzz of their wings. They hovered in place waiting for each ram to show.

They flew in a cyclone motion until the likeness of a man emerged from the eye of the centrifugal force.

"Foul beast, this is your official summons. I am the official representative of the Diocletian Terrestrial Republic, and we rule with the consent of the governed. We have sent messengers requesting your official recognition of the Republic. Denounce your heathen magic and join the almighty Republic and one true faith."

The representative's voice was curt—an unpleasant alto octave.

As he spoke, locusts continued to swarm, "Time and time again these messages have gone ignored. You have exactly three blood moons to present your offering of acceptance to the Republic's capital, or we will make docile that which is wild. As a sample of the Republic's power, we will display the repercussions of defiance."

The herd remained motionless—without control of their faculties. Anti tried his best to avoid detection. The representative wasn't much bigger than Anti. He moved with the arrogance of invincibility. Completely void of empathy, he approached Mya.

Anti noticed the concern in Mya's eyes. She wasn't afraid, but disappointed she wasn't able to protect the herd from a foreign magic—it was her obligation.

The representative gestured, and the cross vanished into locust, dropping Mya's body with a thud. He grabbed her by the hair of her head, placed his forehead directly against hers, and whispered.

"You're not what you thought you were. You're no protector. You're no spiritual guide. Do you want me to tell you what you are?"

He brandished a sword with his free hand.

"You are a failure. A symbol of conquest. When I remove your head from your shoulders, pray they remember you as a martyr as opposed to the failed protector you actually are. That way I can have the pleasure of justifiably slaying the whole lot of you filthy beasts."

Preternatural hearing allowed the herd to hear each word the intruder uttered. They helplessly looked on in horror. All but Anti, he hustled over to the man whose back was towards the crowd. With sword held high, the representative clenched a hand full of Mya's hair.

Anti's thoughts raced as fast as his feet. He had no idea what to do but knew something must be done. Never a victim of fear, he dove on top of Mya as the man brought the sword down in a hammering motion.

Time felt frozen. Anti flinched from the combustion of the sword, but it wasn't with him that the sword made contact. The sword had struck the beetle and hordes of beetles emerged from the slice of the initial beetle. Thousands of beetles surfaced outnumbering the locusts three-to-one.

The beetles violently attacked. As the slain locusts fell, the man slowly disintegrated, and the herd regained control of their faculties. Chaos ensued, triggering a stampede.

Anti clung to Mya as the earth convulsed. Leopold remained on his knees, frozen in shock. Anti helped Mya to her feet. She hugged the boy but wouldn't look into his eyes. Leopold regained his composure and approached the mound. He bellowed as loud as he could, gaining the herd's attention.

"I want the heads of the major families to meet in my tent, immediately!"

In all of the confusion, Anti maintained his distance. He didn't want to be trampled or be the recipient of any misguided anger.

꙾ ꙾

The fervor of the night's ordeal had hardly subsided. A melodic rumbling of low tones and snorts echoed throughout the camp.

Seven rams along with Anti sat in a circle around a log fire. The shadows from the blaze danced along the massive totem pole that stood to the east of the circle. The rams exchanged glances, none revealing their fear until Leopold broke the silence. Anti silently observed.

"It is no secret as to why we are gathered. We must ascertain what provisions we need to exercise for the betterment of the herd," said Leopold.

Anti heard a snort to the right of him from a ram covered in white fur. He appeared as though he could have been Leopold's father, his movements were slower and his shoulders a bit rounded.

"Yes, Sir LieShouer?" questioned Leopold.

"With respect to the crown, we must take a proactive approach."

Before Sir LieShouer could say more, he was cut off by a shorter ram. He was half the height of the other rams and closer to Leopold's age, possessing a brown and white speckled coat.

"Yes! If this attack showed us anything, it's a clear indication that we must seek allegiance. We can not do this alone."

"Honor etiquette!" Leopold said sternly, "only one speaks at a time." He motioned for LieShouer to continue speaking.

"I take no offense, Sprink. I realize enthusiasm and the immediacy of the situation prompted your error. But our sentiments are similar nonetheless. I urge you, Leopold, we can no longer uphold tradition. I know your father's mindset, I spilled much blood alongside your father before his untimely passing. We ruled from a different time ... from a different era. An era when brute force and courage protected us from everything. We could remain a tribe unto our own. This is no longer the case."

LieShouer paused and pointed to the mound in the distance. He then motioned toward the herd.

"Do you hear that?" he asked determinedly, speaking from the top of his chest. "That's legitimate fear. For the first time ever, we have been attacked on our own soil, and we could do nothing about it. We must seek alliance from tribes who have yet to be conquered by the Republic. We need all the help we can gather."

"What help do you presume we need? We were simply caught off guard," Leopold retorted.

The rams desperately wanted to interject, but etiquette would not allow for anyone to display impudence. It would have been interpreted as a challenge for the crown.

A portly built ram began to speak. He had very long horns and a blond coat. "If I may, we were attacked with a sorcery none of us have seen. With all due respect, even the guardian mother—"

Leopold cut him short with a loud snort, "Choose your next words wisely, Justin."

Anti sensed the tension and wondered what he would do if he were King. He knew the heads of the households were right and, deep down, he believed Leopold knew as well. Yet, something was keeping Leopold from making the right decision, and he didn't know if it was pride or if there was something more to it.

"Well ... If she didn't see that attack coming, what makes you think we can see the next?" asked Justin.

"Fair question. We will send scouts out for recon to gather as much information about the Republic as possible. We do not need an alliance. Our lifeblood flows with the tradition of the fiercest warriors the earth has known. No force has ever budged us and no force ever will! We will raise the caution level of the camp and be prepared for war indefinitely."

Everyone at that campfire knew this was a bad idea, but none dared to challenge the King because none dared to challenge the amulet. They now had to place all their hope in Mya, for she was the only one with knowledge of magic.

※ ※

The herd went unbothered through two lunar cycles. They remained on alert but were no longer on edge. According to the herd's rumblings, Anti was being credited for keeping the Republic at bay, undermining the power of the throne. There was not so much as a hint of the Republic's dealing. With each passing day, Leopold grew confident in his decision to remain an independent tribe. He had no desire to dilute his power in any manner, believing an alliance meant compromise and compromise was an action of the weak.

Meanwhile, Mya grew increasingly wary of Anti as time transpired. She alone knew how much power he possessed, but didn't know its nature. She realized she was indebted to him but didn't want that debt hanging over her. She urged her son to off the boy in his sleep, but he insisted the boy was a trophy of the herd. The only way to win back the heart of the herd would be to defeat the boy in a fair duel.

Mya studied Anti closely, but couldn't figure out from where he harnessed his power. He had no jewels, no totems, no incantations—nothing. To her, he was an anomaly, and nothing good came from the abnormal.

The night before the grand duel, Mya entered the King's chamber while Leopold and Anti slept. She desired to speak to the boy without the King knowing. Standing quietly over each, she examined both closely and noticed the same beetle that had attacked the locusts rested on her son's head. Curious, she conjured a spell that allowed her to enter Leopold's dream. Despite her shortcomings with the Republic, she was a powerful sorceress in her own right.

Much to Anti's chagrin, a third energy entered the mind of Leopold. Anti, under the guise of Denascus, sat in a field away from the camp with his legs crossed, meditating. Mya approached her former lover, Denascus, knowing he was an imposter.

"This is where you've been every night? Don't think for one minute I didn't know you were up to something. You're relying on cheap tricks and shoddy sorcery to defeat my son."

Denascus rose to his feet and approached Mya. He stood face to face with his wife. Anti immersed himself fully in the role of Denascus and would not break character.

"Cheap tricks and sorcery? As though you have much margin to speak. Can you recall my, oh so, fortuitous demise?"

"Demise? Cut the crap kid. You're not—"

Before she could finish her statement, Denascus reached back and slapped the Queen's mouth with the back of his hand. To Mya's dismay, she felt every bit of the pain that seared up through her cheek and across her lips. Raising her hand to her mouth, she spat a trickle of blood into her palm, in which she calmly examined.

"How dare you raise your voice to your King! You hornless wench, you are a disgrace in every sense of the word and owe me your life," spewed Denascus with vexation.

Anti took great delight in the theatrics. He was completely engrossed in the role and used that to justify his actions. Mya regained her composure, dismissed the insults and calmly reengaged.

"Yes, my King, your demise may have been fortuitous. Is this the nature of your visit? From the moment you entered the herd's vicinity, I sensed the vengeance harboring within. Yet, I could not understand why a young boy could harbor vengeance toward a herd he had never laid eyes upon. Who sent you, boy?"

Anti wanted so much to reveal his intention but knew if he broke character it would have detrimental ramifications. It was imperative that he, while inside of Leopold's mind, remain true to being Denascus.

"A King's action should never be questioned. The weak explain their actions. As my Queen, you of all people should understand this principle. I've come back for one thing and one thing only, and that's to reclaim my rightful crown and restore the throne. My son will renounce his sovereignty and restore order."

Mya chuckled to herself. She realized Anti was not going to break character, and any escalation of the situation would only further solidify Denascus' impression within Leopold's mind. She opted to bow out with grace. As she turned to leave, she spoke one last utterance.

"I can assure you, no such thing will be done."

❧ ❧

Thunderous percussions awakened the herd on the day of the Grand Duel. It was a festivity. All trepidation caused by the Republic was set aside as exuberance and jubilation filled everyone with joy. The duel was set to begin at the middle sun's apex.

A ceremonial breakfast with live music ushered in the morning's activities. The day prior, Anti had helped gather food. Although excitement filled the air, an undertone of sadness prevailed. The herd had bonded with Anti from the time shared together. In their heart, they did not want the boy to leave. He was seen as a deterrent to the Republic and just the thought of his leaving legitimized their fear.

Leopold relished in the herd's joy. He hadn't witnessed this much fervor since he had claimed the throne. He believed a good showing would win the herd's hearts. He would be respected, not just because of his power, but because of his mercy. He never intended to kill the boy. Truth be told, he had developed an attachment to Anti as well. He considered creating an official position for Anti within the herd's hierarchy alongside, his mother.

Leopold only planned to rough Anti up until he submitted, and then punish the boy for his act of defiance. Bloodshed was out of the question. The boy had saved the Queen's life. He hadn't been sent by the Republic and had proved to be an asset for camp morale.

Custom would have Leopold seek formal blessing from the herd's spiritualist prior to the duel. In his mind, it was more ritualistic than functional.

He performed the ritual near the end of the ceremonial breakfast. Leopold removed a patch of hair from his belly and gave it as offering to Mya before kneeling at her feet. She displayed as much regal bearing as she could, despite feeling insecure due to her deformed horns. She placed her hand on Leopold's forehead and spoke into his mind as he knelt.

"Off the boy quickly. He will be your undoing."

"Mother, I told you the boy is of no threat. In fact, the herd loves him."

"Sometimes you can be so dense. He may be a boy in form, but he possesses a power you can only dream of attaining."

"Mother, why are you over qualifying the boy? He's a boy!" Leopold said with a quiet sternness. He couldn't fathom any threat the boy could present.

"Unfortunately you have underqualified the boy, and it may cost you your life. Did you ever stop to think how a human could make it this far? Did you stop to ask yourself how he scared off the Republic?"

"You suppose, I should have killed the boy immediately? What's done is done. To kill him in any other manner outside of the duel is cowardice."

"I propose you kill him now!"

"Nonsense, we've waited this long. The herd would never forgive me. Besides, he could prove an asset."

"An asset? Better to have a life known as a coward than to not have a life at all. If you spare him, it could lead to a possible rebellion. There are already rumblings about the herd wanting to seek alliance; they already distrust your judgment. You need to kill the boy, now! Your power hinges on it."

"The herd expects a spectacle and a spectacle they shall receive!"

Leopold stood to his feet and kissed his mother atop her forehead. "You worry too much, my dear." He walked away.

As he did, Mya muttered under her breath, "and I'm afraid you worry not enough."

※ ※

As the central sun climbed to its apex, the beat of the war drums could be heard for miles. The herd gathered around the mound. The air carried the stench of musk. As the rams' excitement increased, some butted heads, others stomped their hooves, all were consumed with the spirit of the duel.

Anti struggled to swallow as his throat felt like it was closing. His nerves were setting in. He could barely hear himself think over the commotion. He stood on the mound opposite of Leopold who appeared larger than typical. Anti barely came up to his thigh.

Mya stood between the two gladiators waiting to perform the ceremonial blessing. She approached Leopold and shuddered from the arrogance his aura emanated. She motioned for him to bow and blew a powder into his face. She rubbed his amulet and whispered into his ear.

"Win back your herd, no mercy."

She gracefully hovered to Anti in the same fashion and blew the same purple powder into his face. She bent over as if to whisper in his ear and reached into his pocket. She pulled out the beetle and crushed it within her fingers while whispering, "Good luck."

She smiled and elegantly assumed her place near the base of the mound. Anti tried his best to hide his dismay. The beetle symbolized strength and hope. He now felt naked.

The two approached the center of the mound. There was a barren, oblong-shaped patch of grass. Anti closed his eyes in an attempt to drown out the crowd, and more importantly, his fears.

After they entered, the perimeter of the patch was set ablaze. The flames towered over Anti and caused him to sweat. They eventually subsided to the height of his knee.

Anti opened his eyes and the magnanimity of the atmosphere set in. He inhaled deeply three times and tried to slow his heartbeat. He looked at Leopold and saw him raising his palms in the air, eliciting excitement from the herd— relishing in the energy.

A larger Myer Ram, named Mansa, stepped through the flames. His wool was white with blondish-yellow tips, and he stood slightly less than eye level with Leopold. As a hefty Ram, his voice bellowed. He looked at the two gladiators, turned his back to them and addressed the roaring crowd, motioning for silence.

Anti somehow felt calmed and free of fear, yet, insecure because he was without a solid plan. His hope relied upon the king's vulnerability, and his faith had faltered after seeing the beetle crushed.

Leopold could not be any more confident. He felt in control of the situation. His only doubt came from his ambivalence. He wrestled with the idea of executing the boy in front of the entire herd and the risk of being known as the coward-King and boy-killer. He only wanted to give the herd a unifying event and win back their adoration. Unfortunately, it wasn't only adoration that he lacked, but he'd lost the herd's respect due to his stubbornness. But he trusted his mother's guidance, and he knew she had access to powers none within the herd possessed. If she sensed something, it always turned out to be true—so the boy would have to die.

Mansa sounded a decibel defying horn, then stomped his hooves, beat on his chest and yelled with a bellowing tone.

"THE CHALLENGER ... FROM AN UNKNOWN ORIGIN ... LAYING CLAIM TO NO TRIBE ... STANDING AT A HEIGHT OF TWO AND A HALF WARLINGS, AND WEIGHING IN AT A MEAGER TWENTY-TWO SLAWS. GIVE A ROUND OF APPLAUSE FOR THE ONE WE'VE COME TO KNOW AND LOVE ... AN-TIII-OCH-TI-CUUUSSS!"

The herd unleashed thunderous applause. Anti staggered from the eruption's power. He sensed the love and knew he won the heart of the herd. They appreciated his kindness and courage, and whether they would overtly admit it—each and every one rooted for him.

Anti held back his tears. He finally felt a part of something and didn't want it to end. He knew even if he somehow came out victorious his heart wouldn't allow him to stay, it belonged to the Abyss.

"AND HE IS CHALLENGING THE REIGNING KING! REPRESENTING THE MOST DOMINANT TRIBE IN EXISTENCE ... THE MYER TRIBE. STANDING SEVENTEEN WARLINGS TALL, AND WEIGHING IN AT AN UNDISCLOSED WEIGHT. SALUTE YOUR KING ... LEEE-OOO-POLLLDDD!"

The herd released a thunderous ovation, but the difference was noticeable. The applause lacked passion and was more so out of obligation. Leopold noticed and jealousy germinated within. He shot a cross look at Anti and snorted.

Mansa brought the two opponents to the center of the mound.

"Okay, this is a battle to the death. Anything goes. Magic is barred, I repeat, absolutely no use of magic. Any use of magic will result in an automatic disqualification and subsequent execution. Am I clear?"

Anti nodded while Leopold released a guttural snort.

"Okay, crownsmen. This is a duel for supremacy. Let's get it going!"

Mansa sounded the decibel defying horn again to commence the duel.

Myer Ram's have horrible, nearsighted vision. Leopold looked in Anti's vicinity and only saw a blur. By now, Anti's scent was indistinguishable, so Leopold relied heavily on hearing. He concentrated on the pulse of Anti's heartbeat.

Anti remained perfectly still. Wind gently glided across his flesh, and he thought back to Selma and felt calmed. He thought about reuniting with his mother in the Abyss and felt reassured. He recalled the Mystic River and stood with the quiet confidence that fate would see him through. His aura was a flame in a quiet room—on a solitary candle—left to flicker uninhibited.

Leopold felt anxious because he disliked being encased in fire, the smell of the fire irked him. He concentrated intensely on Anti's heartbeat. He heard it descend from a rapid pace to a slow beat. The boy's calm both frustrated and infuriated him. He released a loud snort, lowered his horns and charged Anti. With commanding and powerful steps, the ground shook with each stride.

Anti had never witnessed anything move with such explosiveness. He intended to move but didn't possess the physical abilities. Luckily, he wasn't tall enough to receive the full impact of Leopold's horns. Unfortunately, he didn't escape being trampled. Leopold's powerful knee drove upward, smashing into Anti's chest creating a loud crack. Anti flew backward, feeling like he was suspended in the air for a lifetime before landing across the inflamed perimeter. He felt shattered all over.

The herd gasped. The duel appeared to be over as quickly as it began.

Leopold faced the crowd and began to pump his arms. He couldn't hide his wry smile as arrogance took over. He snorted loudly and motioned toward the herd.

"Is this the one you cheered so emphatically for? A boy? Look at your boy-King now!"

Mansa reached for the decibel-defying-horn to end the duel, but before he could sound it, Anti whimpered.

Anti's body had been prepared beyond anything he imagined. Selma had reinforced his bones, and the venom from the honey bees of Galoria still pumped through his veins which activated its own magic. Anti whimpered, with a scorched face, he felt his displaced ribs poking through his flesh. Smelling his burning flesh, he remained face down and motionless.

Leopold sauntered towards the boy. Despite the jealousy pervading his thoughts, he had no intention of slaying Anti. He only wished to rough Anti up and provide the herd an entertaining showing. More importantly, he wanted the boy to submit. He refused to be known as the King who slew a child.

He approached Anti with the anticipation of smelling fear and reluctance. Yet, the boy reeked of burned flesh, blood, sweat and reassurance.

Anti's pain overwhelmed his senses. The venom in his blood inhibited his body from going into shock.

"Renounce yourself and your actions, and this will end now. Stand up! I will allow you to give yourself up," demanded Leopold.

Anti struggled to breathe. Short and choppy breaths were accompanied by the piercing pain of broken ribs. He barely possessed the strength to raise a hand, let alone stand.

Leopold looked down at the boy without pity and shrugged. "Suit yourself."

He reached down, grabbed Anti by the waist, and held him above his head like a scepter.

Anti heard a soft murmur from the crowd. The suspense of potentially losing the boy set in.

"Give up now, and this all can be over. This brings neither of us any glory."

Anti did not possess the strength to respond. The blood from his pierced rib trickled unto Leopold's hide. Its acidity burned through Leopold's flesh. He quickly dropped the boy. Anti's face smashed into the mound, knocking him unconscious.

As Anti's blood burned through Leopold's hide, he did his best to conceal signs of pain. He released guttural snorts and stammered.

The herd did not understand what happened but collectively cheered as Leopold wobbled across the ring. They sensed a chink in his armor.

Anti regained consciousness but lacked the strength to stand. His resolve and willpower hardened as he struggled to his feet. He took a deep breath and held it while focusing his energy. As he reached his feet, the herd stomped and roared in excitement.

Anti's blood that seeped into Leopold's bloodstream had an immediate effect. Leopold lost control of his senses. He staggered and stumbled across the mound repeatedly while being singed by the perimeter's flames. His vision blurred, causing him to panic. He lost all sense of smell and could no longer feel. Everything around him darkened as a sense of nothingness pervaded.

Everything was black except a small aura of light. Leopold felt ethereal, as if he was in a dream, and found himself crawling towards the light, who he thought was Anti. He approached and realized the aura wasn't Anti. To his surprise, he was crawling toward the father he had once betrayed.

Anti was accustomed to the mind of Leopold. He knew its outlines very well. He was well prepared for this moment and confidently assumed the role of Denascus. Boldly, he stood with chest bulging and spine arched.

"But ... But ... no ... How could this be? Father? Help me!" cried Leopold.

Anti had no idea how this moment would arrive but seized advantage of the opportunity. He felt no physical pain, for his thoughts were completely submerged inside Leopold's delusion.

Leopold continued to crawl towards his father, trembling in a hysterical panic. He embraced his father's legs as he did when he was a runt lamb before he was given the amulet.

"Father ... please forgive me for my betrayal. I need your help. It was the woman's idea—mother made me conspire against you. It was all her."

Denascus knew this was a lie. Leopold spoke only out of a need for survival.

"Where is it?" demanded Denascus.

"Where is what?"

"The dagger you used to pierce my heart."

Leopold kept the dagger concealed at all times so no one would stumble across the evidence. The narrative that was painted was that Denascus had been poisoned by his wife-to-be, Selma. The truth was, the poison hadn't killed him. It had merely weakened him. The dagger that was impaled through his heart finished him off.

Leopold withdrew the dagger from his breastplate and placed it at his father's feet.

"Father forgive me. I was but a coerced child, following his beloved mother's commands."

"Did you show me mercy when I lay there unable to move—pleading for my life?"

Feeling contrite, Leopold lowered his head.

"Make right the error of your ways and return to me what is rightfully mine," demanded Denascus.

Leopold removed the amulet without hesitation.

"Here my King, what's yours shall be returned." Leopold handed the amulet to Denascus. As soon as the amulet hit Anti's hand, vibrancy exploded throughout his body. The magic began to accentuate and amplify within Anti. Leopold's stature diminished until he became Anti's size—reduced to the runt he always was.

Even though the entire ordeal took place within Leopold's mind, it dualistically effected reality.

The herd remained stunned in silence as they witnessed Leopold hand Anti the amulet, and were even more shocked by Leopold's diminutive size. The amulet evoked Anti's internal magic and allowed his body to mend itself.

Denascus held within his grasp the very blade that had taken his life.

"I understand what must be done, Father. I just wish there was another way. No one should have to bury their child." Leopold attempted one final plea to play on the emotion of his father.

The plea fell on deaf ears. Anti was on a mission—a boy seeking to fulfill a destiny, and nothing could deter him.

Anti raised the dagger.

"Fath—"

The strike of the blade interrupted Leopold's plea.

Leopold's skull landed on Anti's foot and rolled across the grass. His body hit the ground, and because of the silence, the boom echoed. The amulet enhanced Anti's stature, and he appeared to double in size.

The herd gasped in disbelief. They were prepared to lose a King today but had no idea it would be Leopold.

Mya buried her face in her palms.

Questions flooded throughout the herd. "Was it magic?" If there was magic involved they couldn't discern. "Was the boy now King?" There was a steady murmur until Mansa sounded the horn.

The crowd erupted into a deafening roar.

"Rooot, rooot, ROOOT!!" The crowd graciously welcomed their new King.

"AN … TI … AN … TI … AN … TI!!" The crowd began to chant repeatedly as they rushed the mound. The mass pushed through the fire and raised Anti above their heads.

※ ※

Anti relished in his glory for only a night. He stayed an additional night for the ceremonial crowning and informed the counsel of major families that he would need to leave and wasn't sure if he'd return. They offered to send two scouts with him, but he declined. He knew he could not be the King that the herd desired, at least not at this time.

His fate belonged with the Abyss, and even the prospect of power couldn't deter him. On the morning of his departure, Anti prepared his belongings. He took with him the amulet, the dagger of the fallen King, as well as the skull of Leopold.

He left the herd with some hope. He explained that he may return and take up the throne one day. In the meantime, he suggested that they allow the counsel of the major families, along with the spiritualist, to guide their actions.

Anti looked upon the King's throne and fell to his knees. He wept, and it took him some time to regain his composure. The time he'd spent with the herd had been his most enjoyable moments outside of time spent with his mother. He heard the familiar buzz of the beetle, watched it fly to the throne, contemplated staying, but dared not to defy fate.

As he looked around the King's chamber one final time, Mya entered. She hovered towards Anti. He didn't know what to expect. He hadn't spoken to her since her son's demise and anticipated the worst.

"King, I commend you."

"Huh?"

"I warned my son. I will be honest with you. If I were him, you would not have lived past the first night."

Anti inhaled deeply.

"But now we have an outsider as King, I will not accept it. While you are gone, I will do everything in my power to erase your memory."

Anti now stood eye level with Mya. Fully confident in himself, he smirked and walked out of the tent. He turned before exiting, which captured Mya's attention.

"Oh ... and Selma sends her regards ..."

Mya closed her eyes and bit her lower lip as all the pieces fell into place.

❧ ❦

As Anti approached the forest, the wind blew violently while trees swayed back and forth. Anti sensed the forest was reacting to his return. Selma felt Anti's presence days before he reached the forest's vicinity.

His aura had expanded exponentially since he'd last seen Selma. When he arrived, she was the first to greet him with a warm smile.

"Boy, you've grown," she eyed Anti up and down, "It seems like so long, but it's only been a blood moon."

Anti was relieved to see her and felt like a weight had been lifted. His excitement was infectious, and Selma sensed his eagerness.

She hugged him with a firm embrace, grabbed the boy-King by the hand and led him through a portal to her den.

Exhausted, he needed rest but anxiously wanted to disclose his adventures to Selma. It was as though he was returning to his mother after a long summer retreat. Upon entering the den, he lay down and stretched out his elongated limbs on the carpet.

"I did it! I really did it!" he said with exuberance. He caught Selma off guard, even though she viewed him as a child, there was always a layer of ruggedness that shielded his innocence. But now, his tenderness completely bled through.

She analyzed the boy's enlarged body, "You must be tired, come have a seat. I've prepared supper for you."

Selma was impressed by how quickly Anti's aura had amassed. She sensed his power was on par with hers. While she prepared his stew, he shared his events.

He connected with her mind's eye.

"Impressive," she mumbled, Anti had a control over his mind that she didn't expect.

Anti sensed the satisfaction and elation she felt by witnessing the events unfold. Her happiness transmuted her aura, and Anti's eyes widened as her appearance began changing. An auburn mane sprouted from her head that contrasted her fern-colored fur. Her ivory bones slowly covered with auburn fur as her muscles gained a meaty thickness. For the first time, Anti saw Selma radiate, she was happy—genuinely happy.

"Oh Anti, you are now the boy-King. What a wonderful journey you've endured."

'This is for you." Anti removed the amulet from his neck and handed it to Selma. As he did so, his size reduced to its original form.

"No, I couldn't take this from you. The amulet is with its rightful owner. You have restored my peace. Our debts are cleared."

Anti blushed, "No, please. You must," while Anti handed the amulet to Selma, he noticed a small vibration in his pocket. Selma grinned. He reached into his pocket and smiled as he felt the reassuring flutter of wings.

"You see, even when you give away what's rightfully yours, a piece of it always finds a way to stay with you," said Selma.

"If that's so, shouldn't you be on your throne at the Myer Camp?" asked Anti.

The question stung. Selma often wondered what life would be like back at camp, but didn't believe rejoining was possible. Anti's conviction and resolve convinced her that anything was possible.

"Perhaps you're right, Anti," she said, handing Anti a bowl of stew, "but that's another story for another time. Eat up, you need to rest. You have an Abyss that needs finding."

Anti ate and reflected on his journey. He couldn't believe it all. It felt like he was dreaming. After he finished eating, Selma motioned him to the back room. Anticipating his return, Selma had knitted him a blanket to use for the night. Before he retired, he reached into his pouch.

"I have something else for you," he pulled out the skull of Leopold and gave it to Selma. He felt she needed a trophy of justice.

Anti didn't realize she was storing his memories for that very reason. Seeing Leopold's face brought painful memories flooding back. She hugged Anti, to shield her tears from him. She was happy, and the possibility of returning to her tribe began to germinate.

Unbeknownst to Anti, magic had a way of draining the soul that the user wasn't always aware of. Selma knew he needed to be restored. Selma let him fall asleep and induced a deeper slumber. A slumber that lasted an entire blood moon. While he slept, Selma crafted a crown for him using Leopold's skull. There was a power in a Myer Ram's skull that she did not want him to be without.

Anti awoke in a haze to see Selma standing over him. He had no idea how long he had been sleeping but was fixated on one thing—the Abyss. Anti's face beamed as he placed the crown Selma had created onto his head. He felt an immediate surge in his conviction—his entire purpose for being where he was—for being who he was—the motivation of it all. His earnestness emanated as an aura of its own and caused Selma to shield her eyes.

"Selma—"

"I know child; it is time for you to continue your journey."

"Yes, but do not take it as a slight against you and your company," replied Anti.

"I do not. Fate has a special way of keeping us all on track."

"You are more than welcomed to join me."

"Anti, I'm afraid this is a journey for one. Besides, I do not know where the Abyss is. There is a reason I have never seen it, and I never will."

"But ... you were to help me?"

"Yes. I will keep my word. The Abyss isn't a physical place that can be seen by all. The Abyss is a physical plane that must be manifested by one's mind's eye," said Selma.

Anti contemplated. He couldn't rationalize the concept, but it resonated with his spirit.

"You have everything within yourself to find the Abyss. You simply must go," said Selma.

It was as though Anti departed in that very moment. His mind had already left. He just needed to prompt his body.

He spoke his condolences, gave thanks to Selma for all she had done, exited the forest and headed east. He didn't know what the result of reaching the Abyss would be, but he felt he would see Selma again. Yet, he had to find the Abyss and reunite with his mother.

He walked for an entire blood moon, undeterred, and without seeking food or water. He walked until his legs no longer allowed him to do so. His mind outlasted his body.

Anti felt the rays of three suns beating down on him. He was so far within his mind that he didn't feel his legs give out. Slumped, lying on the desert floor with blistered lips, his mind continued to roam. His mind continued traveling, but he remained trapped within his body—stuck in darkness.

He cried out.

"Mother ... Mama ... Mom!"

Sporadically, he cried out, "Selma ... Mama ... Selmama," his body no longer responded to any of his commands. He felt a wiggle in his pocket.

The beetle crawled from his pocket. His eye twitched in response to the prickly sensation of tiny legs crawling past his sternum to his forehead. It nestled on top of his forehead and flapped its wings. Anti's eyes burned and began to water as he lost his vision.

Vertigo set in, and he could no longer discern up from down. He felt like he was falling while the world simultaneously spun chaotically.

Anti gathered all his strength to cry out, "Help! Mom!"

"I'm here ... stand and open your eyes," a soft voice retorted.

Reinvigorated, Anti stood and opened his eyes expecting to see his mother, but what he saw was even more of a wonder. The Abyss appeared like a mirage bursting through the night's veil. Anti had witnessed nothing grander. It stretched forever in both directions. He hurried to the edge to seek the source of the voice but saw no one. Immense heat waves proliferated from the bottomless void. The Myer Ram's skull allowed his flesh to endure the torridness, and the venom within his veins kept his blood from boiling.

"Mother?" Anti yelled into the Abyss, "Mama, where are you?" He yelled and yelled but heard nothing. The prospect of never seeing his mother again began to constrict his aura. His entire purpose felt like a lie.

Anti placed his toes over the edge of the Abyss, tilted his head to the side, and looked down. A tear cascaded down his cheek, falling into the emptiness. He felt like his destiny had died, yet fate seemed to be pushing him in a different direction.

Anti drove back both the hope and despair that flooded his aura. The beetle stopped fluttering its wings and silence inundated.

Anti sensed fate staring into his soul. He stared back, looking over the edge, only seeing bottomless forsaken destinies. The beetle detached from his forehead and plummeted into the Abyss. Impulse pleaded for Anti to dive after, and he succumbed. He had nothing left but his trust for the beetle. It had guided him thus far. Without fear and overwhelmed by ambition, he leaped.

Time practically stood still. Anti saw the entire span of time; it was as though he was hovering outside of time. He could see time's future and past, and witnessed many truths.

Still, he fell. As he continued to fall, destiny and magic concerted to reconstruct Anti's fate. The beetle crafted an aura specifically for Anti that both time and magic found an affinity for. Anti spun in a spherical motion as an aura was being forged around him. He poked a liquid filled sac that he was enclosed in and watched the beetle crawl along the outside of its fragile membrane.

Anti suddenly felt frozen, his body, his thoughts—everything. The sac continued to fall, until it crashed, bursting open. Anti spilled out. Sticky, he stood to his feet and eyed his surroundings. The process of falling had felt like an eternity, but now it seemed as though the entire ordeal had taken but an instant.

He was back where he started—at the edge of the Abyss, with a renewed sense of purpose. He knew now who he was—the Restorer. It was he who would restore things to their proper balance, and restoring is what he would do.

The Abyss showed him the universal law, the significance of order, and why the two must stay balanced. Even if this meant watching the world burn to begin anew.

Antiochticus the Restorer was born.

ĀKASYA ẞENGE

Akasya Benge has lived in Tokyo, Istanbul, and New York, and has a bachelors in literature from Ursinus College and a masters in art history from New York University.

She now lives in Delaware with her beautiful cat and many, many plants and waits for the day she can live in a house full of stained glass windows.

Other than writing, she sometimes illustrates her own stories, which you can find on her website:

thecitadelstudios.com

Or her Instagram: @thecitadelstudios.

Natural Enemies is her debut short story.

ANDREA HARGROVE

Andrea is a librarian in Eastern Pennsylvania. This is her first published work, but she is looking forward to more in the future.

JACK E. MOHR

Jack E. Mohr is from Spring Valley, California. He graduated from Morehouse College with a bachelor's in Business Administration-Management, where his desire to write came to fruition. Jack is self-taught and enjoys studying and developing his craft daily.

His real passion is sci-fi/fantasy using creative writing to explore alternate universes while delivering thought-provoking stories that inspire the imagination of readers.

Jack's first published short story, *Dodson*, can be read in the *Fall in Fantasy* anthology by Cloaked Press. His second short story, *Thank You for Calling* can be read in the *Second Chance* anthology by Zimbell House.

Jack can be contacted via:

Instagram (@TheArtofJack) or (@JackWritesMohr)
Blog (ingloriousresurrection.com)
Twitter (@JackWritesMohr)

DAWSON LEE HOLLOWAY

Dawson Holloway has been an aspiring writer ever since he was seven, after meeting local writers such as Christopher Paul Curtis and writing several Star Wars adventures.

Now, at nineteen, he has developed quite the repertoire and is ready to enter the publishing world. He attends Oakland Community College to save some money (though he plays tuba with the Oakland University Band) and writes whenever the urge calls to him.

EZEKIEL O. TRACY

Ezekiel O. Tracy is an artist, baker, and writer. He wrote his first book when he was ten and has pursued writing ever since. With several self-published novels, and short stories in anthologies such as *Smaerelit Volume 3*, and the online publication, *Dreaming Spirit Press*, Ezekiel is following his passion. He lives in Ohio with three cats.

Ezekiel O. Tracy has written and published the novels *The Death* Diary and *River & Pauline*. You can follow his project The Other/s at www.ezekielotracy.wordpress.com

J.T. SIEMS

JT Siems is the owner of Immortal Perfumes, a micro-perfumery specializing in historical scents. When she's not crafting perfume oils based on Dead Writers, she enjoys writing fantasy and steampunk novels.

Siems lives in Seattle with her husband, toddler, and evil cat.

JESSICA SIMPKISS

Jessica lives and works in Virginia Beach, Virginia with her husband and daughter. She is a graduate of George Mason University.

Her work has most recently been published, or is forthcoming, in *Beautiful Losers, The Bookends Review,* and *The Dead Mule School of Southern Literature.*

KRISTIN TOWE

Kristin Towe is a student of literature, a writer of poetry and fiction, and an occasional fairy chaser.

Her most recent work appears in Z Publishing's anthology *Georgia's Best Emerging Poets*.

LESLIE D. SOULE

Leslie D. Soule received her M.A. in English from National University. She is a scholar, artist, citizen journalist, and martial artist. She has been an established writer for a decade.

What sets her work apart from the pack, is its intensity in dealing with the ultimately personal journey of life and its myriad setbacks and sorrows. Her novels contain a deeply populist, anti-establishment tone, one in which rebellion against the often-authoritarian norm is praised. Her work embraces the outcasts of society—the discarded, the rebels, the people that the magazines forgot to tell you exist.

Readers enjoy Soule's no-nonsense, fast-paced style of writing. She loves to hear from her readers, encourages them to connect with her on Twitter and to help spread the word about her work.

Other Anthologies from Zimbell House

The Fairy Tale Whisperer
The Mysteries of Suspense
Garden of the Goddesses
Elemental Foundations
Romantic Morsels
The Steam Chronicles
Pagan
Tales from the Grave
The Adventures of Pirates
Curse of the Tomb Seekers
Travelers
Dark Monsters
On a Dark and Snowy Night
Where Cowboys Roam
The Key
Veil of Secrets
Tournament Games
The Lost Door
Nocturnal Natures
It's an Urban Style of Love
The Neighbors
Date Night
Why? A Collection of Mysterious Tales
The Mountain Pass
River Tales
After Effect
Morsels from the Chef
Ghost Stories
Second Chance
Children of Zeus

A Note from the Publisher
How to Thank a Contributor

Dear Reader,

Everyone at Zimbell House Publishing would like to thank you for reading *A Nymph's Tale*. If you would like to thank a particular contributor, the best way is to leave a review for them. You may do so by leaving one on our Goodreads page, under the *A Nymph's Tale* title, by using the link below and be sure to mention the contributor directly:

http://www.goodreads.com/ZimbellHousePublishing

Why should you leave a review? Reviews help budding authors build their credibility in the book industry. By posting a review on Goodreads or other sites, you help other readers find new authors they may wish to follow, and you never know, your review may end up on an author's website one day.

Friend us on Goodreads:
https://www.goodreads.com/ZimbellHousePublishing

Follow us on Facebook:
https://www.facebook.com/ZimbellHousePublishing/

Follow us on Twitter:
http://twitter.com/ZimbellHousePub